DAZZLING EMOTION . . .

Without another word, he caught her hand and pulled her to her feet, but when he would have placed his hand at her waist, she reminded him that they stood upon a gravel walk. "We cannot dance here, for I am wearing slippers."

As Matthew looked into her upturned face, her brown eyes were alight with teasing laughter and her mouth quivered from the attempt to contain a smile. Her eyes were beautiful, but it was that quivering mouth that held his attention and shot a bolt of lightning through his blood. His gaze focused upon her soft lips, and it was all he could do not to gather her in his arms and cover her mouth with his own.

"I give you fair warning, minx. Forsake your saucy ways, or I shall be forced to do something we might both regret."

"And what might that be, sir? Oblige me to dance barefoot on a bed of nails?"

"Madam," he said, tugging at her hand to bring her a step closer, "I warned you."

The
Artful Heir

Martha Kirkland

A SIGNET BOOK

SIGNET
Published by the Penguin Group
Penguin Putnam Inc., 375 Hudson Street,
New York, New York 10014, U.S.A.
Penguin Books Ltd, 27 Wrights Lane,
London W8 5TZ, England
Penguin Books Australia Ltd, Ringwood,
Victoria, Australia
Penguin Books Canada Ltd, 10 Alcorn Avenue,
Toronto, Ontario, Canada M4V 3B2
Penguin Books (N.Z.) Ltd, 182-190 Wairau Road,
Auckland 10, New Zealand

Penguin Books Ltd, Registered Offices:
Harmondsworth, Middlesex, England

First published by Signet, an imprint of Dutton Signet,
a member of Penguin Putnam Inc.

First Printing, April, 1998
10 9 8 7 6 5 4 3 2 1

To Diana Cruz,
who was a friend to my child
when a friend was needed.

Chapter One

"My reason for traveling to Northumberland," Sarah Sterling replied to the plump, middle-aged lady whose gray sausage curls bounced beneath the wide poke of her pomona green bonnet, "is to do a job of work."

Her inquisitor was the only other passenger not to quit the stagecoach at Newcastle upon Tyne, and she seemed to think their continuing together, being jolted and tossed about as the coachman urged the four horses over the rough terrain, granted her special license to ask all manner of impertinent questions. "You must be a governess, then, my dear. I thought as much when first I saw you climb aboard in London."

Sarah vouchsafed no reply. Her clothing was plain enough—a Manila brown traveling dress, a tobacco brown pelisse, and an unadorned straw bonnet—to mark her as a governess or a paid companion, and though she aspired to neither post, she allowed the woman to assume whatever she wished. It mattered little what some stranger might think. One thing only was of importance, that Sarah not be turned away once she reached Donmore Hall. She must not be denied this employment. She must not! So much depended upon it.

The last two clients had refused even to consider her, never mind her qualifications, and now she had

come to the north of England, almost to the Scottish
border, hoping to fulfill the last of her father's con-
tracts. It was the very remoteness of Bellingham that
had led Sarah to hope she would not be sent packing.

"What is the name of the family to whom you go?"
the woman asked. "I am persuaded I shall know
them. There are not, after all, so many families in the
district that any are unknown to me." She made a
sound that in a younger woman might have been de-
scribed as a giggle. "It is true what people say of
Northumbria. The sheep do, indeed, outnumber the
people."

Sarah could well believe the truth of that statement. Having traveled for four days and covered
more than two hundred and fifty miles, she had been
witness to some rather dramatic changes in landscape as well as in population size.

After beginning their journey at the Red Lion, the
stagecoach had rattled its way through the ever-
crowded, noisy streets of London, heading north
through the nearby countryside. The first real scenic
change came as the stage passed through the grassy
downs—with mile after mile of pretty farms and or-
chards. Next came the gentle rolling hills and valleys
of the Midlands, where the shimmering waters of the
beautiful Ouse River surprised the traveler around
first one turn and then another.

The farther north they traveled, the terrain grew
less gentle and they encountered fewer people. Finally, the heavy coach had reached the Pennine
Chain, where it slowed considerably, lumbering
through the wild, beautiful scenery of the rugged
mountains and quiet lakes. Drystone walls had replaced the hedgerows of southern England, and
everywhere small, shaggy sheep roamed about
searching for coarse grass to supplement their diet of
heather.

"The sheep do seem to be plentiful," Sarah said, skirting her fellow traveler's question regarding her destination. "And I do not believe I have seen a human for fully an hour."

"No," agreed the woman, "not since we passed that stone cottage where the pale blue anemones grew right up to the door."

Sarah had not noticed the flowers. She was much too interested in the four little children who had rushed out of the cottage to view the coach, waving and calling to the passengers as they passed, excitement on their young faces as though they witnessed a raree-show. "Where people are few and diversions rare, I imagine the passage of the stage is an event."

The woman nodded, making her fat curls bob like two tightly wound springs against her plump cheeks. "In the north country, one is obliged to take one's entertainment where it may be found. As for society, we are obliged to be much more democratic than might be the established mode in more populated areas. If it were not so, those of the great houses—of which there are but three in my particular neighborhood—would have no one to make up the numbers when a dinner party is got up."

Warming to the subject, she continued. "In Bellingham, which is my home, Lady Edwina Camden-Reynolds is the only *real* nobility. The daughter of an earl, she is married to Mr. John Reynolds of Sykes Manor. As for titled gentlemen, there is but one in the neighborhood, and though Sir Harold is only a baronet, Fairlie Park is every bit as pleasant an establishment as Sykes Manor. However, Donmore Hall is the largest estate, with the greatest number of tenants, which makes its owner, the new heir, the most important gentleman. If gentleman he may be called." She lowered her voice as though concerned that they might be overheard. "There are those who say the new owner of the Hall is not—"

"Damnation!" yelled the coachman, his curses slicing through the woman's gossip. "Hellfire!"

An instant later, a shouted warning came from the box. "Look out there, you idgit!"

Hard on the driver's words, the coach swerved to the right, threatening to toss the passengers to the floor. To save herself, Sarah grabbed at the leather strap beside the squabs and hung on for dear life. For an eternity the coach seemed to slide sideways, then it swiped against the stone wall and the sound of splintering wood rent the air. After several bumpy moments, the vehicle lurched to a stop, and the woman with the curls was flung unceremoniously across Sarah's lap.

"Heaven help us!" the woman screeched.

Sarah had managed to save herself from serious injury, and though her fellow passenger made almost as much noise as the horses—their high-pitched screams indicative of their panic—that lady's maltreatment consisted of nothing more than a crushed bonnet and wounded pride.

Perceiving that little harm had come to herself or her traveling companion, Sarah pushed the woman none too gently back into her seat and bade her be quiet for a moment. "For I have heard not a sound from the driver."

After several moments had passed and nothing was heard from the coachman, Sarah opened the door. "Best stay here, ma'am, while I see what has happened." Ignoring the woman's pleas not to leave her, Sarah climbed down into the road.

Pandemonium reigned. The coachman lay slumped on the box, not moving, while the team neighed and tossed their heads in fright. They probably would have been running at full speed that very moment if the harness of the lead horse nearest the wall had not been caught fast between some stones, forcing them to remain.

The beast's eyes rolled in a manner that told Sarah he needed attention immediately, before he did himself permanent damage. However, she was not a fancier of horseflesh, and with little experience of the breed, she was understandably reticent to get too close. Not knowing what to do, she looked about her, wondering how she was to free the animal while still keeping as much space as possible between herself and those powerful hooves.

To the rear of the coach, Sarah spied the cause of the entire debacle. An animal—the strangest she had ever seen—was just now jumping to the other side of the wall. It was a bull, of that much she was certain, but its kind was questionable, as it appeared more ox than cow. Its body was long and rather lean, and its thick head was adorned with short, curved horns, but those were not the weirdest features. Oddly enough, the bull's pelt was a ghostly white, and for just a moment Sarah gave in to the foolish fancy that the creature was not of this world.

Knowing she could not stand there gawking at the animal, she moved with caution toward the team. She had almost reached them, when she heard a masculine voice from somewhere to her left.

"Do not dither about there like a half-wit!" a man yelled. "Either grab the horses' bridle, or get out of the way where I can jump the wall without landing on top of you."

She turned immediately to discover a gentleman on horseback. Tall and well built, the man sat astride a spirited chestnut that he held in check by sheer brute strength.

Happy to accept help of any kind, she ignored his animadversions upon her wits. "I should much rather you dealt with the team, sir. My experience of horseflesh is limited."

"Then move aside," he ordered.

While Sarah hurried toward the rear of the coach, the rider turned his horse and galloped back across the field. After making a circle, he urged the chestnut forward at full speed. Sarah's heart seemed to beat in time with the pounding hooves, though it all but stopped when the horse bunched its powerful muscles and sprang upward, leaping over the stone wall. Man and beast glided beautifully, almost effortlessly through the air, as though they had taken wing.

It was the work of a moment for the rider to dismount and go to the team. Speaking softly, he first caught the near leader's cheek strap, then while he stroked that animal's forehead with long powerful-looking fingers, he inched toward the more frightened horse on the off side. Continuing in the same unhurried manner, the man soothed the second animal with his voice and his competent hands, all the while reaching around toward the crevice in the stone wall where the trace had been caught.

"There's a good boy," he crooned. "You have had a scare, but everything will come right. Here's my word on it."

Sarah had no idea whether or not the horse believed the assurance, but she did. Something about the man convinced her that he did not issue promises, or threats, unless he was prepared to follow through on them. Broad and muscular, he weighed at least twelve stone, and the way he carried himself fairly screamed, "Proceed with caution."

He had discarded his beaver hat, leaving it on the wall near the chestnut, and his dark brown hair shone in the afternoon sunlight. Worn rather longer than was fashionable, the thick, crisp hair brushed the collar of his bottle green coat. The gentleman's skin was quite tanned, as though he had spent most of his adult life out-of-doors, and seeing him at closer range, Sarah suspected he might be a bit younger than she had originally guessed, possibly no more than thirty-two or -three.

When she was certain the man had the team under control, Sarah lifted her skirt several inches, tucked the fullness up under her pelisse out of her way, and climbed up onto the box to see to the coachman. The driver had not moved, but she had heard him moan once or twice.

"How is he?" the gentleman asked.

She had not realized the man was watching her, and she blushed to think she might have exposed her legs to his scrutiny. "He has a bump on his forehead," she said, "but I think he is coming around."

As if to verify her diagnosis, the driver moaned loudly and struggled to sit up. "What's amiss?" he muttered groggily.

"All is well," Sarah assured him. "The other passenger and I are unhurt, and a gentleman has come to the rescue of the team." She lifted her gaze, looking past the four horses. "Are they fit, sir?"

"More frightened than injured," he replied. "If driven slowly, I have no doubt they can cover the two miles to Bellingham without suffering any adverse effects. Can the same be said of the coachman?"

Sarah looked into the ruddy face of the driver. His skin was ashen beneath the years of windburn, and his eyes seemed disinclined to focus. "I think not, sir. I believe we might all come to harm if someone else does not handle the horses."

The gentleman hesitated only a moment, looking behind him at the chestnut that waited farther down the lane. Turning back, he surprised Sarah by instructing her to take the ribbons.

She gasped. "But I cannot control four horses! Not even for two miles."

"I had not supposed that you could," he answered in an exasperated voice that made her feel as though she had been tested and found wanting, "I merely asked you to hold the reins. Will you oblige me by doing as I requested?"

Fighting a combination of embarrassment and anger, she found the reins where they had fallen across the dashboard. She caught them securely between her fingers, then she straightened on the box. "I have them," she said with more confidence than she felt.

Not certain what she had expected, she watched the gentleman catch hold of the leader's mane and vault up onto the horse's back. "I shall ride postilion," he said, "you need only hold the ribbons firmly so they do not fall to the ground and confuse the team."

Without waiting for her reply, the man tapped his booted feet on either side of the animal's flank, and the team began to move forward at a gentle walk, the stage lumbering slowly behind them. In a little less than half an hour, they entered Bellingham, a medieval town with narrow cobbled streets and a market square.

For the most part, the dozen or so shops were composed of brick, but a few were fashioned of red Cumbrian sandstone. At the top of the high street, just past the inn yard, stood a gray stone church. Primarily of thirteenth-century design, the handsome building had incorporated some Anglo-Saxon features, though what caught Sarah's attention was a structure just to the rear of the church. Standing proud and tall on the hallowed grounds was a perfectly preserved fourteenth-century *pele* tower, a common type of fortification begun to be built after the Normans arrived.

If the events of the last hour had not left her too dis-
mayed to smile, Sarah would have done so upon spying a fortified vicarage, standing as if ready to do
battle with the ancient Scots.

It was not to be wondered at that half the town
filled the street before the stagecoach came to a stop
beneath the sign of the Mute Swan. If the vehicle
alone was enough to send children running to their
cottage doors, who could blame the adults for being
interested when the coach offered the spectacle of a
lady on the box holding the ribbons and a gentleman
riding postilion?

"Sir," said the red-haired young ostler who ran to
the horses' heads. The first to arrive within speaking
distance, the lad was obviously too stunned to think
of a question befitting the occasion, so he contented
himself with repetition. "Sir."

"The team took exception to one of our Chilling-
ham cattle," the gentleman said, as though in answer
to a sensible question, "and as a result, the far leader
got too close to the stone wall. He has sustained a
nasty cut, so see he is given every care."

The lad pulled his forelock. "Yes, sir."

"You there," the man continued, motioning toward
a pair of likely looking shopkeepers who had come at
a run to see what was happening, "go to the other
side and help the driver down from the box. He has
been injured as well."

While the two shopkeepers did his bidding, the
gentleman swung his long leg over the horse's with-
ers, being careful not to get caught in the tack, then
he slid to the ground with an ease that would have
been envied by a real postilion. Taking several pur-
poseful strides, he stopped beside the front wheel
and held his arms up to Sarah. "Down you come," he
said.

With the gathering crowd watching her with eyes

wide and mouths agape, Sarah felt her face grow
warm with embarrassment. When she had climbed
up to the box, she had given little thought to how she
would get down. However, even if she were capable
of alighting with the skill shown by the gentleman,
she doubted she could have done so with several
dozen pairs of eyes watching her every move.

Girding herself with what little composure she
could muster, she set the reins aside and stood, hoping with all her might that a ladylike method of
reaching the ground would present itself. Her hopes
went unfulfilled, and as she looked down at the
ground, all she could think of was how very far away
it appeared.

Her apprehension must have shown on her face,
for with a muttered oath, the gentleman climbed up
to meet her. Standing on the iron rung that served as
a footboard, he reached toward her, and before Sarah
knew what he meant to do, he had caught her around
the waist and swung her clear of the box. He ignored
her gasp of surprise, and brought her close against
his chest, his arms holding her fast.

"Wrap your arms around my neck," he said, "and
hold tight, for I will need the use of at least one of my
hands if I am to get us both down in one piece."

Sarah had, perforce, to comply with his request,
though when she had hoped for assistance, this
rather intimate method of dismounting had not figured as her first choice. Being swung from the box in
such an unladylike manner, with her skirts and petti-
coat flying about her every which way, had brought
warmth to her face, but that warmth was not to be
compared to the scorching heat that rushed through
every inch of her as a result of being in a man's firm
embrace, with her arms around his shoulders and her
body held flush against his.

Only a few inches separated her face and his, a circumstance that prompted Sarah to close her eyes, welcoming the illusion of distance fostered by such a craven act. Unfortunately, nothing could disguise the feel of his muscles bunching and rippling as he climbed from the coach. To her relief, their proximity lasted but a few seconds, and the instant her feet touched the ground, she pulled free of his hold.

"I, er, thank you, sir, for your assistance."

Chancing to look up into his face, Sarah encountered an unholy light in his gray eyes, and she had the most unsettling feeling that he was trying not to laugh.

"Think nothing of it," he said. "Believe me, the pleasure was all mine."

Before she could decide if he was making sport of her, or if she had imagined the whole, he made her a careless bow then turned and walked away. The crowd parted like the Red Sea, allowing the gentleman to move unimpaired. As he passed them by, the women all curtsied and each man either tipped his hat or touched his forehead. A few bystanders murmuring greetings, though for the most part there was silence.

"Well," said an angry voice from inside the coach, "must I remain here all day, or will someone offer me assistance?"

As if galvanized by the petulant request, everyone began to speak at once, while one of the shopkeepers rushed to open the coach door and assist the middle-aged woman with the sausage curls to alight.

"Please, be careful of that one," Sarah advised the ostler. He had dropped her portmanteau on the ground as though it were a bag of feed and was now reaching for a rather odd-shaped wooden box with leather corners and handle. Not that she had any real confidence in the state of the contents of the box, not after the way the stagecoach had bounced around. Still, the leather-trimmed container held the means of her livelihood, and if the bottles were broken or spilled, the question of whether or not she was given employment would be a moot point.

"Are ye being met, miss?" the young fellow asked.

"I am not, and I will need transportation to Donmore Hall."

The lad's face turned as red as his hair. "T'hall, miss?"

"Yes. Do you know the place?"

"Yes, miss." As if to prove his case, he pointed a rather grubby finger toward the uplands some mile or so east of the village. Nestled between two pine-covered hills, the greenery so dense it was almost black, was a large sandstone house. Even at a distance the structure was impressive.

"What a view the inhabitants must have."

The lad shrugged his shoulders. "Wouldn't know, miss. I never been up there."

Suddenly beset by thoughts of Bluebeard's castle, Sarah asked him if he knew the family. "You are acquainted with Mr. Donaldson, are you not?"

"Oh, aye, miss. And old Mr. Donaldson before him."

Reassured, she said, "I look forward to making the gentleman's acquaintance."

At that, the ostler turned even redder than before.

Not wanting to jump to conclusions again, she said, "Is something the matter?"

"Nothing, miss." The lad ducked his head. " 'Cept you done met him."

Sarah was growing weary of the fellow's blushes and cryptic remarks. "Whom have I met?"

"Mr. Donaldson, miss. The new Mr. Donaldson, that is. Him as brought the stage in."

*   *   *

Donmore Hall was as impressive up close as it had been when viewed at a distance. Sarah had never seen anything quite like it, for the handsome three-story edifice was built around the hall of a beautifully preserved, black stone Norman castle, with the newer structure—possibly no more than a hundred years old—fashioned of red Cumbrian sandstone. The combination of colors had mellowed over the century to a union that was quite pleasing to the discerning eye of an artist.

"Lovely," she said.

The taciturn groom who drove the pony cart made no reply; he simply urged the slow-moving old roan mare to continue. A quarter mile farther down the lane they came upon a wrought-iron gate set in a stone wall the same black as the ancient hall, and since the gate was open, the mare plodded her way through. However, once they were on the gravel carriageway, the groom drew the pony cart up beside a small, sandstone gatehouse.

Though they could not see Donmore Hall from that particular spot, due to the meandering of the long gravel carriageway around a stand of ancient holm oak trees, the driver stared in that direction as though he could.

"Your pardon for asking, miss," he said hesitantly, "but you want I should stop at the front door?"

Clearing his throat as though embarrassed, he added, "My brother, as works in the stables, says when old Mr. Donaldson were alive, all save the gentry went around back to see Mr. Angus Newsome at the steward's office."

Like the driver, Sarah looked in the direction of the Hall, imagining she could see the imposing recessed entrance, with its massive double doors. Aware of just how tenuous was her claim to be here, she chose to follow the established mode. "Take me to the steward," she said.

She was, after all, a hired worker—at least, she hoped to be hired—and in her position she dared not offend the sensibilities of the master of the house. One never knew what sort of reception to expect. Even her father, who was one of the most respected art restorers in Europe, tread softly on the issue of his place in the hierarchy of these great houses. Occasionally he was afforded the respect due an artist of his caliber and treated as a guest in the house. However, more often than not he was viewed by master and servant alike as of no more consequence than the seamstress hired to come in and see to the mending of the bed linen.

The driver, apparently relieved not to be stopping at the main entrance, urged the overfed old roan forward. Within a matter of minutes, the mare covered the half mile or so to the house, then continued on the carriageway as it meandered to the left around the far side of another stand of oak trees. As they drove by the oaks, a soft breeze stirred the shiny blackish green leaves, and Sarah fancied they whispered to her that she had come on a fool's errand.

Refusing to listen to such negative thoughts, just as she had refused to heed the doubts that had plagued her during the long, exhausting trip to Northumberland, she gave her attention to the unexpected view from the rear of the house. Beyond the neat tile-roofed stables, the land rolled gently downward, providing a dramatic view of the distant hills and vales that were covered by a dark green spruce forest.

Sarah found the rugged beauty hauntingly appealing, and to her list of reasons why she hoped she might remain at Donmore Hall, she added another, that she might be given the opportunity to capture on canvas the scene before her.

While she looked her fill of the untamed landscape, the driver stopped the pony cart beside a cobbled footpath that led from the stables up to the rear of the house. "The steward's office be just there," he said, pointing to a door that gave access to the corner room where the path began.

After accepting the promised shilling for his services, he jumped down from the divided seat and went to unload Sarah's battered portmanteau and the leather-trimmed box strapped to the back of the cart. Meanwhile, Sarah drew the strings of the reticule that matched her brown faille pelisse and returned the purse to her wrist.

Alighting unaided from the cart, she straightened her bonnet and turned resolutely toward the steward's office. She had taken only a half-dozen steps in that direction when the door was flung open and a slightly built man dressed in a serviceable gray coat and flocked waistcoat came outside, a beaver hat and a riding crop in his hand. Apparently unaware that he was not alone, he stopped short when he saw Sarah.

In his late forties, he was so close to Sarah's own height that she fancied she could look directly onto the top of his head, where his thinning salt-and-pepper hair had been carefully combed to conceal his pink scalp. Though far from handsome, he might have been pleasant-enough-looking under normal circumstances. At least, Sarah hoped these were not normal circumstances, for at the moment the skin around the man's left eye was black and blue and the lid all but swollen shut; in addition, his bottom lip was split in the corner and appeared painfully puffy, and a large, angry bruise colored his chin.

"What the devil!" At his quickly spoken oath, the man gasped and put his free hand to his mouth, obviously regretting having moved his lip injudiciously.

Sarah tried to ignore the poor man's face. It was evident that he had been in an altercation, and judging by his relatively unscathed knuckles and the lack of cuts or bruises on the back of his hand, he must have gotten far worse than he gave.

"Mr. Newsome?"

At his nod she said, "I am Miss Sarah Sterling, and I am here to fulfill a commission my father accepted from Mr. Matthew Donaldson."

The man looked at her as if he had no idea to what she referred, the dull green of his uninjured eye showing little interest in her or her story. "What sort of commission?"

Sarah tried for a confident air. "We received a letter from Mr. Donaldson requesting the services of an art restorer. Unfortunately, my father is ill and unable to travel such a long distance at this time. Therefore, I have come from London in his stead, prepared to execute the needed cleaning and restoration to the Donaldson collection."

At the mention of the collection, the steward appeared more interested, though his tone was still far from friendly. "You say the request was for your father's services?"

This was the moment of truth, and Sarah took a deep, fortifying breath, praying all the while that she would not be sent away simply because of her gender. "I have worked at my father's side for years, Mr. Newsome, and I have ample experience as a restorer. Furthermore, I have come a not-inconsiderable distance, prepared to begin work immediately. As for the new inventory of the collection and the verification of the authenticity of a number of the paintings, I am qualified for both those tasks as well."

For just a moment, surprise showed on the steward's face—surprise and something else—though Sarah had the feeling his reaction had nothing whatever to do with her being a female. While she waited, he lowered his gaze, successfully hiding his thoughts, and when he looked at her again several seconds later, his expression revealed nothing.

"I wonder that Mr. Donaldson did not apprise me of your expected arrival," he said, his tone much more affable than before. "Did you, perchance, bring his letter with you, Miss Sterling?"

"Why, yes. I did."

"May I see it?"

"That will not be necessary," said a voice from just behind her.

Even before she turned, Sarah knew to whom that voice belonged. Had she not heard it scarce an hour ago?

Once again the tall, dark-haired gentleman was astride the spirited chestnut, and as before, he stared at Sarah as if the encounter was more an annoyance than otherwise. She had, perforce, to look up at him, and though not as happy to see him as she had been earlier, when she had been unaware of his identity, she squared her shoulders and gave him look for look. He was master of Donmore Hall and, she hoped, her new employer, and if she had any chance of remaining in Northumberland, she felt certain she must not let him see how disconcerted she was at his sudden appearance.

"Good afternoon, sir. You are, I gather, Mr. Matthew Donaldson."

"And you," he said, his tone not at all conciliating, "are *not* Mr. Garrick Sterling."

Not allowing her an opportunity to respond, he spoke to his steward. "Newsome?"

The little man inclined his head in what might pass for a show of respect. "Yes, sir."

"Have someone escort the young lady to the book room. I will join her there presently."

Matthew Donaldson's words were spoken softly enough, but there was no doubting the authority behind the voice. The man was obviously accustomed to giving orders, and just as accustomed to having them carried out to the letter without hesitation. If Sarah were to make a guess, she would say the gentleman had been in the military, and watching him ride toward the stable, his broad back straight, only strengthened that suspicion.

Angus Newsome opened the door he had exited only moments before. "Come," he said, "the book room is just beyond my office."

They passed through the steward's domain so quickly Sarah had time to note little else but a battered desk made of deal pine, a cabinet of some sort, and a ladder-back chair. Within seconds she was being led down a short, uncarpeted corridor and ushered into a handsomely appointed library.

"In here, miss."

It was a large book room, twice as long as it was wide, with ample space to accommodate a massive oak desk, a glass-fronted vitrine, several comfortable-looking red leather chairs, and row upon row of book-lined shelves. On either side of the fireplace, French windows opened onto a small square of lawn, beyond which stood the holm oak trees the ostler had driven past earlier.

Too nervous to sit, Sarah walked over to the vitrine to have a look at the three miniatures on the top shelf and the dozen or so porcelain pieces below. She believed Angus Newsome had let her into the room and had then left her there, so when he spoke, she jumped.

"You appear to be more intelligent than the average female," he said.

Sarah turned to look at the man who stood in the doorway. His words were hardly a compliment, and she did not pretend they were. "I like to think I need not blush when in company."

"That's as may be. All I know is, you'd be wise to heed my warning."

Liking this conversation less and less, Sarah said, "What warning is that, Mr. Newsome?"

"Do not remain here at Donmore Hall, Miss Sterling. Believe me, 'tis no fit place for a decent woman."

Chapter Two

"And why is it not a fit place?" Sarah asked. "Do you tell me that no decent females are employed here? No maids, no sculleries, no laundress, no—"

"I don't mean the servants," he interrupted, his manner impatient, "they've the housekeeper to watch out for them, not to mention their own families as near as the village. You've no one to protect you."

Protect me? From what?

Sarah experienced a moment of uncertainty, but her need for employment overrode any qualms she might have. "This is foolishness," she said, wishing her voice held more conviction. "Mr. Donaldson is a gentleman, and surely—"

"Him?" Newsome's top lip pulled upward in a sneer. "He's no gentleman. Ask anyone. They'll tell you right enough."

With that invitation, the steward inclined his head, backed into the corridor, and closed the door, leaving Sarah standing in the middle of the book room, her brain reeling from this latest information.

"He is right, you know. I am no gentleman."

With the opening of one of the French windows, a gentle breeze wafted into the room, but it failed to cool Sarah's cheeks. She was warm with embarrassment at having been caught gossiping. "Sir, I—"

He silenced her with a wave of his hand. "Never mind, Miss Sterling. I am aware of the sentiments of both my servants and the villagers. They had hoped for a more . . . shall we say, refined heir."

His broad shoulders lifted in a negligent shrug. "Unfortunately, life is filled with unrealized hopes and expectations. A circumstance with which a female obliged to earn her living is no doubt acquainted."

"Well acquainted, sir." Sarah swallowed with some difficulty, for this interview could not have started more inauspiciously.

"Then you cannot be surprised to hear that I am disappointed your father was unable to comply with my request for his services. The job that needs doing requires an expert."

"He complied with the request, Mr. Donaldson. The expert he sent is me. And while I am well aware that many people are reticent to trust a member of my sex, please allow me to assure you that—"

"Acquit me of any such bias, Miss Sterling. I spent the last fifteen years in the army, and for the first six of those years I was a trooper of the line, slogging through snow in winter and knee-deep mud in summer, with nothing between me and certain death but my wits, my Brown Bess, and what I carried in my knapsack. Oddly enough, the times I came closest to losing my life were those when I was obliged to obey orders issued by some half-wit *gentleman* whose purchased commission gave him the right to tell me how to fight."

Sarah could only stare. Fifteen years? He must have been only a lad when he enlisted. Poor boy, he—No! She had problems of her own and no time to waste feeling sorry for Matthew Donaldson. No matter what his childhood circumstances or his army experiences, he was now a wealthy man, with a fine house, a sizeable art collection, and a bevy of servants to wait upon him. Surely such amenities must serve to soften even the harshest of memories.

Whereas *she* had nothing but her proficiency as an artist to—

"As a result of my experiences," he continued, "I have no great respect for the supposed intelligence of my own sex. Therefore, I feel no inclination to make a blanket assumption about the supposed lack of intelligence in females."

"Then . . . then you will give me an opportunity to prove myself? Oh, thank you, sir."

"Save your gratitude, Miss Sterling, for I made no such promise. Your ability notwithstanding, it is out of the question for you to remain here. Newsome's advice, however unflattering to me, was nonetheless valid. I am a bachelor, and the reputation of a decent woman would not survive even one night's stay at the Hall."

Sarah was totally unprepared to confront such an argument, and fearing that her chances for employment were slipping away, she grabbed at the first thought that occurred to her. "What you say is probably true, sir, for a lady of tender years. However, since I am not all that young, I am convinced that no one will regard my being here. You may believe me when I tell you that no one notices women of a certain age."

"Women of a certain age? What nonsense is this?" He looked her over from her bonnet down to her half boots, then back up again. "You can be no more than nine-and-twenty."

"Six-and-twenty!" she answered much too quickly. The moment she said it, she saw the light of devilment in his eyes and knew he had tricked her into the confession.

"Just as I thought," he said. "I can give you seven birthdays and at least a hundred years of experience of the world, and you may believe me, Miss Sterling, you *would* be noticed."

Hoping to divert the feeling of panic growing inside

her, she lifted her chin defiantly. "I care nothing for what others may say of me."

"Ah," he said, "very brave of you, I am sure. But what if I care what they say of me?"

"Pshaw! You are a man. And a wealthy man at that. You know as well as I do that in this world, such men may say and do what they please."

As he looked at her, his right eyebrow lifted in a way that said he questioned the logic of her argument. "An interesting assumption, ma'am. However, in such cases as this, where young ladies are left unchaperoned with said wealthy men, one often hears of irate fathers and brothers who suddenly appear, weapons in hand, to show the fellow he is not so immune to the conventions as he supposes."

This was plain speaking indeed, but since Sarah had more or less introduced the subject, she was determined not to turn missish now. "I have no brother, sir, and my father is unwell, so you need have no fear that by employing me you will ultimately find yourself forced into parson's mousetrap."

"I do not fear it," he replied. "Only a gentleman would bow to such social coercion. As I said before, I am no gentleman."

"Then why—"

"I merely wished to show you the fallacy of your generalization that wealthy men might do as they liked."

"I stand corrected, sir. Pray, allow me to go from the general to the particular. I need this job too much to let the fear of gossip send me home."

"Nonetheless," he began, "I do not think it prudent for you to remain here, so I am afraid you must—"

"How about this?" she said hurriedly, before he could refuse her unequivocally. "What if I sign a paper saying you have apprised me that you have no desire to be forced into matrimony, and that I have agreed to make no demands upon you, no matter what the outside provocation."

That right eyebrow lifted again, but he seemed to be considering what she had said. While she waited for his reply, he looked her over again, only this time, it was no cursory glance from bonnet to boots. This time, those cool gray eyes made a slow perusal of her figure, lingering rather long upon the swell of her bosom before wandering to her hips then sliding from her thigh to her ankle. "And what of provocation from within?" he asked, his voice suddenly low and seductive.

Sarah knew he was trying to frighten her, and though heat had followed the journey of his eyes back up her body, leaving a betraying dampness inside her collar, she vowed to remain calm.

Not finished with her, he said, "What if I should find you too tempting to resist? What if the very sight of you day after day brings out certain animal lusts within me, lusts so depraved they prompt me to make passionate love to you?"

"Why, then," she said, untying her reticule and withdrawing from its depths a short pocket pistol, "I should be obliged to put a hole through you."

For just a moment, as he stared down the double barrel of the small but lethal weapon, Matthew was taken aback, though after turning his attention to the serene face of the young woman who brandished the pistol, he threw back his head and laughed. "Is that thing loaded?"

"Not at present," she replied pleasantly.

"You are certain?"

"Quite," she said, returning it to its brown faille home and drawing the strings once again. "My father insisted I carry the pistol for protection on the road, and to give him peace of mind, I agreed. However, since I was obliged to keep it in my reticule, I chose not to load it." Her smile held just a touch of embarrass-ment. "I was afraid it might fire accidentally and sep-arate me from one of my toes."

"A wise move, ma'am."

"Lest you think otherwise, sir, I am perfectly capa-ble of both loading and firing the weapon. Just as I am perfectly capable of caring for your art collection, which is, I understand, quite extensive."

"Correct," he said, allowing her to turn the conver-sation.

"And in need of cleaning, restoring, and verifying for authenticity."

"That, too, is correct."

"May I see it?" she asked.

Matthew hesitated. He wanted to deny her request, yet something stopped him from uttering the words. Foolishness, surely, for from the moment he had dis-covered who she was, he knew he could not let her stay at Donmore Hall. He needed an art expert—the need was immediate and pressing—yet as soon as he heard Miss Sterling identify herself to Angus New-some, Matthew knew he must send her back to the vil-lage. For all concerned, it was best that she pass the night at the Mute Swan, then be put upon the stage-coach that passed through on the morrow.

The collection be damned! There was no place in his house for young ladies; just as there was no place for them in his life. He had no knowledge of such women.

While still a boy, and shy of the fair sex, he had gone from the halls of Eton directly into the army. As the years passed, and softly rounded bodies began to fill his dreams, the only females who would spare a moment for a soldier of the line were anything but ladies. Since the tavern girls seemed to enjoy Matthew's company every bit as much as he enjoyed theirs, he saw no reason to seek more elevated companionship, not even after his bravery won him a battlefield commission.

Now, here he was owner of a great house and custodian of a king's ransom in art, and suddenly young ladies were being introduced to his notice, matrimony the obvious object of such introductions. Because he had no intention of paying court to any of those damsels, he had scrupulously avoided all but the most public encounters.

The new master of Donmore Hall could not contemplate marriage to some gently reared female. He knew, even if they did not, that his manners were those of a rough soldier, and since he could not bring to the Hall the kind of woman he was accustomed to, his fate as a bachelor was sealed.

Miss Sterling obviously mistook his hesitation, thinking it an indication of his lack of confidence in her ability, for she walked over to the vitrine, opened the glass-paned door, and removed the three miniatures that reposed on the top shelf. "Since these are in your book room, I assume you like them. Am I correct?"

"You are."

She placed the oval portraits faceup on the oak desk, the pink-cheeked child first, the gentleman with the powdered hair next, and lastly the elderly woman with the deep-set, pensive blue eyes. "Do you know anything about the artists?"

He shook his head.

"What of the paintings?"

Keeping his knowledge to himself, he said, "I know that I like them. Especially the—"

"No," she said, holding up her hand for silence, "do not tell me which you like best, allow me to tell you."

"What is this, some sort of parlor game?"

"It is no game, sir, for I take art and artists seriously.

This is merely a way to demonstrate to you that I am informed on the subject."

Intrigued, he folded his arms across his chest and waited for her to begin.

"This one," she said, indicating the young man, "was painted about fifty years ago by Richard Cosway, a friend of the Prince Regent. It is one of his earlier works, and though charming, lacks the fine brush stroke of his later years."

She lifted the miniature of the child. "And this was done perhaps thirty years ago by Marie Cosway, Richard's wife. There are those who believe her work superior to his. In this instance, at least, I agree."

"And the old woman?" Matthew asked.

"Yes," she said, lifting the delicate portrait and holding it to the light so the blue of the eyes fairly shone. "This is your favorite."

"You are quite certain?"

She smiled, and Matthew noticed that hers was a rather entrancing mouth, with the upper lip finely drawn and the lower lip full and soft-looking.

"Quite certain," she said, bringing his thoughts back to the portrait. "You could not help preferring this one, and rightly so, for it is the work of Nicholas Hilliard, the recognized master of the miniature. It is also the most valuable piece of the three. Though it still retains its vibrancy, and is in excellent condition, it was painted at least two hundred and thirty years ago."

"Very impressive," Miss Sterling."

Matthew knew little of art, but he had looked up those three pieces in the old inventory done more than a quarter of a century earlier. Her facts might have been read directly from those pages.

She had stated her findings with complete confidence, and she did not undermine her credibility by

inviting him to verify her words. Instead, she asked
once again if she could view his collection.

"Not now," he said.

"If not now, when?"

"After you have had your tea," he said. Having uttered the words, Matthew knew the decision had been
made. Though he might live to regret it, he was going
to allow Miss Sarah Sterling to remain at Donmore
Hall.

He walked over and pulled the cord to summon the
butler. "I will have Bailey show you to your room."

She sighed as though she had just set down a heavy
load. "Thank you, Mr. Donaldson."

"Save your gratitude. You will no doubt be cursing
me when you see the work that needs doing."

She shook her head. "I look forward to it."

A knock sounded on the door, and after permission
was given to come in, a tall, middle-aged butler entered the room.

"Yes, sir?"

"Show Miss Sterling to the yellow bedchamber."

If the very proper servant was surprised to be asked
to show to the best guest room a person hired to do a
job of work, he kept his opinions to himself and his
face impassive. "It shall be as you wish, sir."

"And, Bailey?"

"Yes, sir?"

"Choose one of the maids to attend to our guest. Inform the servant that she is to sleep in the dressing
room as long as Miss Sterling is in residence."

Matthew spared a moment to glance at the lady's
face. There was an instant's surprise there, then a look
of relief that was quickly hidden by her lowered
lashes. Though correctly interpreting that look, he
made no comment, waiting until she was at the door
before he spoke again. "Miss Sterling?"

"Yes," she replied, turning to look at him.

"I will expect you in the gallery in one hour, ready to work."

"I will be there."

"And Miss Sterling?"

"Yes?"

"That item in your reticule?"

"Yes, sir?"

"See to it first thing. You might yet have need of it."

Chapter Three

Ten minutes before time to meet her employer in the gallery, Sarah began preparations to quit the beautifully appointed bedchamber with its pale yellow bed hangings and its muted yellow-and-blue Axminster carpet.

"You want I should unpack your things, miss?" asked the young maid, Morag, who had brought her a cup of strong tea and two hot buttered scones.

"No!" Sarah replied rather quickly.

The servant was little more than a child, with the soft, rather musical accent of the north country and wide button black eyes set in a thin earnest face. At Sarah's sharp tone, her features grew even more serious. "I'd be that careful, miss. You'd have no cause to worrit none, for I'm quick to learn and willing to please. Ask anyone in the house, they'll tell you."

Sarah felt like an ogre. She had not been certain if Matthew Donaldson was serious about her needing the pistol, so she had loaded it, then tucked it away in a drawer of the dressing table. The last thing she wanted was for the maid to yank open the drawer and cause the weapon to fire.

"I have no reservations about your abilities, Morag, and I should be pleased if you would unpack for me. First, however, there are some things I wish to store in the dressing table—some items I need for my work. These items belong to my father, and when he entrusted them to my keeping, I promised I would not let anyone else handle them."

"Of course not, miss. I understand. You want I should come back later, after you've had a chance to see to your fa's things?"

Sarah nodded. "And thank you again," she added when the maid opened the door, "for the lovely tea. I cannot tell you how much I enjoyed it."

Blushing with pleasure, the girl bobbed a curtsy and left the bedchamber.

Happy to be alone at last, Sarah finished her tea then unfastened her portmanteau and removed an item wrapped in a protective oilskin. It was a book—her father's reference book of colors—and the formulas written on the pages contained in that small volume represented years of diligence and patient experimentation on Garrick Sterling's part. To an art restorer, the value of such a reference was inestimable, but because it represented the life's work of her father, it had added value for Sarah.

Not certain she would be given an opportunity to restore any of Matthew Donaldson's paintings, she put the book away safely with the pistol inside the drawer. Once that was done, she prepared herself to begin her employment. After washing her face and hands, she combed out her burnished red hair and wound it into a simple knot, then she changed her traveling costume for an unadorned frock of pale green muslin.

Like all her work clothes, the frock was easily laundered, and in addition to the crisp white apron she tied around her high waist, she also filled in the low neckline with a lawn guimpe. The necessity for that last cover-up she attributed to the coolness of the northern clime, and *not* to her employer's warning about the possible emergence of his animal lusts.

The yellow bedchamber was in the east wing, above

the steward's room and the book room, affording a breathtaking view of that area beyond the stables which Sarah had admired when she first arrived. However, when she reached the gallery, which was at the front of the house, directly over the hall, she discovered an equally impressive view from those north-facing windows. In the foreground was the charming village of Bellingham, while beyond the village stood windswept grassy hills so majestic they might have been carved by the hand of a master sculptor.

The natural scenery, lovely as it was, could not hold her attention for long, however, for the pictures hanging on the muted cream walls of the gallery beckoned to her. Paintings, large and small, covered almost every inch of space in the long gallery, with smaller works grouped around larger ones, size being the criterion for the groupings. The creations of the old masters hung above, below, and beside those of the newer masters, and as Sarah glanced around the room, she was unable to believe the vastness of the collection.

There were portraits by Holbein, Eworth, and Lawrence. Landscapes by Hollar, Turner, and Constable. Works by Van Dyck, Lely, Rubens, Sir Joshua Reynolds, and many others. So awed was she by the scope and the variety that she stood transfixed—unmoving as the Bernini bust that rested upon a pedestal near the door—unaware of anything or anyone save the display of genius all around her.

It was while she stood thus that Matthew entered the room. He was not surprised to find Miss Sterling all but spellbound, for he had experienced much the same reaction when he first beheld the collection. Even though he knew little of art, he had felt bemused upon first entering the gallery, the greatness of the work speaking for itself. For an artist, he supposed the effect must be staggering.

Because Miss Sarah Sterling had eyes only for the

works upon the walls, Matthew allowed himself a leisurely perusal of his new employee. She was both more and less than he had expected. Free of the somber brown pelisse and bonnet, she was far more comely than he had originally thought. At the same time, dressed as she was in her simple green frock, with an apron tied around her trim waist, she appeared less like one of the young ladies introduced so eagerly to his notice and more like one of the village lasses.

He had noticed her pretty brown eyes earlier, also the neat, slender nose and the well-shaped mouth, but at that time he had not seen or even guessed at the beauty of her hair. Though fashioned in a simple knot, the deep reddish brown tresses were thick and shiny, and unpretentious curls fought their way free of the confines of the knot to frame her temples and the nape of her neck.

With the hair uncovered, her complexion appeared creamier, the wide brows more expressive, the lashes darker. As for her person, the heavy faille of her pelisse had been unable to disguise completely her feminine curves; still, Matthew was unprepared for his reaction to the slender figure revealed by the softly draped muslin. Heaven help him! She made him remember he was a man, and that it had been months since he had spent an evening in the company of a comely female.

Whoa, old fellow! This particular female is here because you have need of her knowledge. Any other needs, you would do well to put from your mind. And the sooner the better!

He had no more than admonished the animal within when the object of his attention discovered him watching her. "Sir," she said, still too enthralled by the paintings to notice that her employer was ogling her like some callow youth, "I am speechless. The collection is so much more than I had anticipated. Why, it must rival that of the Duke of Buckingham."

"Upon that fact, I cannot comment. All I know is that the Donaldsons have been putting their money into art for several centuries. Fear of the marauding Scots, no doubt."

"The Scots? I do not understand."

"Portable wealth," he replied. "When one is obliged to flee the enemy, the land is, of necessity, left behind. Not so with paintings. What could be easier than to remove half a dozen or so of the most valuable canvases from their frames, roll them up, and stuff them into one handy valise? Who would notice them tucked between the shirts and the handkerchiefs?"

She gasped as if horrified by the thought, and Matthew chuckled. "I see you think me a Philistine, Miss Sterling, for even suggesting such measures."

"No, sir. I was merely taken aback by the idea. The possible damage resulting from such handling of a centuries-old canvas is too frightening to contemplate. Who would have the nerve to do such a thing?"

Matthew looked away from those naive eyes. "Who, indeed?"

Not wanting to address that particular subject at present, he suggested they walk the length of the room. "There is an inventory of sorts," he said, "but it is not the most recent, I am afraid. The newer one seems to have vanished about the time of my cousin's demise. I am hoping you can bring the records up-to-date."

"I can," she said without hesitation. There was no boast in her assertion, simply a statement of fact that she could do the job.

As they progressed to the far end of the room, she paused occasionally, looking closely at first one then another of the canvases. Many were hung too high for her to give more than a cursory glance, but when they reached a small, though vibrant Rembrandt—a study of a young soldier—she stopped. After examining both the bottom corners, she turned to look at Matthew, concern writ plainly upon her face.

"Sir," she said, "the previous owner—"

"Mr. Carlton Donaldson," he supplied. "My father's first cousin."

"Do you know if the gentleman was of the opinion that all these canvases were originals?"

Matthew did not answer her question, but posed one of his own. "Are you of the opinion that they are *not*?"

She blushed, but the color was not due to embarrassment. It was compassion, and if the reticence in her eyes was anything to go by, she hated to tell him what she had found.

"Is that not a Rembrandt?" he asked.

"Not completely," she answered softly.

"You mean it is a fake?"

She shook her head. "Not exactly."

For just a moment, Matthew wondered if he had erred in trusting this job to her. "Let us have no roundaboutation, Miss Sterling. A thing is either real or it is not."

"With art, sir, such things are not always so easy to determine. Not always black and white, if you will forgive the pun. The work is Flemish, and it was most certainly painted under the master's tutelage. In fact, his brush stroke is detectable just there."

She pointed to the shadowed helmet held beneath the soldier's arm. "The bleeding of color at the two joined planes is done with a minimum of brush strokes to maintain the vibrancy. Yet the brushwork is almost rough, with the strokes appearing rather prominent around the two blended areas."

Matthew looked where she pointed, and though he

knew little of the painting process, he saw what she was explaining.

"Now," she continued, "look there where the beard touches the tunic. Can you see the difference in the techniques?"

To his surprise, he could see it.

"Rembrandt painted the helmet," she said. "Someone else, possibly a protégé, created the rest of the portrait."

"Hence," Matthew said, "it is, and it is not, a genuine Rembrandt."

"Still, sir, it is a beautiful painting. And though not as valuable as you might have hoped, it is nonetheless, a joy to behold. And a treasure."

She pointed to another canvas, one showing a large view of London after the great fire of 1666. "That, however, is not a genuine Hollar. Nor is it even a particularly good copy."

He looked from the painting to her. "How can you be certain?"

"For one thing, though the varnish has been smoked to simulate age, I estimate the paint beneath to be no more than thirty or forty years old."

"Then my cousin was duped?"

"He, or perhaps the dealer he trusted."

Sarah spoke softly, worried that her findings might have caused her new employer pain. "I am sorry, sir, but such things do happen, as more than one unwary collector has discovered. I hope you are not too disappointed."

"Not for myself," he said, surprising her.

"For Mr. Carlton Donaldson then?"

He shook his head. "I never met the gentleman. For most of my life, I was not even aware of his existence. He and my father were estranged—probably over money."

Far from embarrassing him, this piece of family history brought a sardonic light to his eyes. "My parent, a lighthearted rogue who was liked by one and all, lived by his gaming skill when his luck was good and by borrowing from friends and acquaintances when his luck was out. As you can imagine, such men, no matter how charming they may be, do not endear themselves to their relatives."

Anyone hearing the indulgent tone of Matthew Donaldson's voice would have no trouble in discerning that *he* at least had found his roguish parent endearing.

"As for Donmore Hall," he continued, his manner serious once again, "since it was not entailed, I never expected to be heir to it or to the collection. And if anyone knows why everything was not bequeathed to the gentleman who for years figured as old Donaldson's heir, they have not informed me of the particulars.

"The facts notwithstanding, everything was left to me, and I consider it a trust, something to be protected and maintained for future generations. I have accepted that guardianship, Miss Sterling, and to that end, I need to know immediately which of the paintings are genuine and which are not. And, as much as it can be determined, I should like to know which of the fakes bear more recent paint."

Something in his voice set off alarm bells inside Sarah's head. This was no idle request. "Sir, if you will forgive an impertinence, did your relative's illness require that he be confined to his bed? And if so, for how long?"

Her employer gave her a slow, studied look. "You are very astute, Miss Sterling. I believe I must congratulate myself on being wise enough to retain your services."

Obviously that was to be her only answer, for without another word, Matthew Donaldson walked to the door. Before he quit the gallery, however, he turned and told her he would send the old inventory to her immediately. "For the moment, I should like a new one as quickly as possible. Where you are not certain of a painting's authenticity, merely state your doubts and go on to the next work."

"But, sir. Such a slapdash—"

He silenced her with a wave of his hand. "I realize such half measures must offend your pride, Miss Sterling, but I wish you will humor me. It is important that I have a workable inventory without delay. After I have such a document in my possession, you may take as long as you like to reaffirm your earlier findings."

"Mr. Donaldson, do you suspect that someone is—"

"I suspect," he said, "that you will need help removing the heavier paintings from the walls. I shall instruct Bailey that you are to be given the services of a pair of likely lads. Anything you need—no matter what it may be—you have only to ask. Your wishes will be given first priority."

With that, he left the room, closing the door behind him. After he left, Sarah stood in the middle of the gallery, looking about her at the numerous paintings.

"What is this about?" she asked, as if hoping one of the portraits might come to life and answer her question. Nothing quite so dramatic occurred, but the longer she thought about it, the more convinced she became that Matthew Donaldson believed someone had been substituting copies for original works of art.

Sarah did not see her employer again until several minutes after the final dinner gong had sounded. She had heard the first gong, but not certain whether she was to take her meals in the dining room like a guest, or on a tray like an employee, she had not returned immediately to her bedchamber. When at last she entered the room, she found Morag pacing the floor nervously, waiting to help her dress.

"La, miss," the girl said, hurrying to the washstand to pour steaming water from a brass can into a pretty, rose-edged ceramic washbowl, "did you not hear the dressing gong?"

Sarah looked at the large carved oak bed, across which lay her cream sarcenet. It was an unpretentious gown, with small, puffed sleeves and a square neck, but it was the only gown she had brought with her suitable for the occasion. "I must have been too en- grossed in my work to hear anything," she lied.

"The first gong sounds at quarter past," Morag in- formed her, "the second at five minutes to, then the last on the hour. Since the dressing gong went a full ten minutes ago, you've little time to freshen up."

Sarah showed the maid her hands and arms, which were filthy from handling long-undusted frames. "I am persuaded that freshening will not serve. Nothing short of a good scrub brush will do for this grime."

The maid tsk-tsked. "Such dirt, miss. Were you working in the gallery, or in the garden?"

"You may well ask."

While Sarah removed her filthy apron, then allowed the girl to help her out of her muslin frock, she recalled the afternoon's work. It had been as exhilarating as it was dirty.

Only minutes after Matthew Donaldson had quit the gallery, the butler had entered it, followed by a pair of footmen carrying a large deal worktable and a chair with a braided leather seat. "I have brought ink and paper," Bailey said, "and you've only to tell James and Henry which pictures you want taken down, and they will see the job done."

Thus had begun her first three hours of employ- ment.

Using the quill and paper supplied by the butler, Sarah first drew a grid of the far wall, filling in squares, ovals, and rectangles to represent the pictures that hung there. In one corner, the muted cream walls showed outlines where four small pictures had once hung, and in the interest of thoroughness, she included those four shapes in her drawing. Once she had assigned a number to each of the shapes, she allowed the footmen to remove the topmost row of pictures, setting them on the floor in order, just beneath their usual places.

Resisting the urge to send for dust cloths, she listed on a separate sheet of paper the number assigned each piece, the artist's name—or in at least one instance, the supposed artist—then the title or a brief description of the scene or person depicted. After number three had been examined, Sarah gave up trying to keep herself clean. So engrossed was she in her work, that only when the gong sounded did she notice the failing light.

"Here's the drying cloth," Morag said once Sarah had soaped and scrubbed her hands, arms, and face until they tingled. "Soon as you're dry, if you'll take a seat at the dressing table, I'll brush out your hair."

Sarah declined the offer, choosing instead to brush her own hair, making short work of twisting it into its usual knot and securing it atop her head. Stepping into the dinner dress was the work of a moment, and once the tapes and hooks were secured, she fastened at her neck her one piece of jewelry, a delicate gold chain bearing a teardrop-shaped garnet.

"You look a picture yourself, miss, if you'll forgive me saying so. And such a pretty necklace."

"It belonged to my mother."

Not wanting to discuss her mother, whose death from the influenza was still as painful today as it had been more than a year ago, Sarah grabbed up her paisley shawl, thanked Morag for her help, then hurried toward the grand staircase. Her foot had just touched the top step when the final gong sounded, announcing dinner.

All but running down the broad stairs, she was still a bit breathless when the footman ushered her into a handsomely appointed drawing room. Matthew Donaldson stood at the far end of the room, near a Chinese Chippendale table upon which reposed a decanter of sherry and several glasses.

"Your pardon," she said, "for being late. I—"

She stopped in the middle of her excuse, for to her surprise, the gentleman who returned his glass to the table was not her employer. Though every bit as tall as Matthew Donaldson, the similarity ended there, for the stranger was three or four years younger, blond-haired, blue-eyed, and quite slender. Every inch the town beau, the young man wore a corbeau coat and gold patterned waistcoat whose exquisite cut spoke the hand of Weston of Conduit Street, London.

"Good evening," the gentleman said, executing a graceful bow.

Not a little flustered, Sarah made a curtsy that was not nearly so graceful. "Good evening, sir. I had no idea Mr. Donaldson was expecting guests."

"I was not," came an icy voice from behind her.

She turned to find her employer just inside the doorway, appearing dark and handsome as Satan himself in a burgundy coat worn over a cream marcella waistcoat. He stared directly at the visitor, his brow lifted in question. "The butler did not inform me of your arrival, sir."

The stranger came forward, his hand outstretched in welcome, almost as if he were master of the house and Matthew Donaldson the guest. "I pray you, cousin, do not take Bailey to task, for he has known me since I was in short coats. You must know that I have run tame at Donmore Hall all my life."

"Cousin?" Matthew took the proffered hand,

though his manner was less like a host and more like a dog whose territorial boundaries were being challenged. "We are related then?"

"In a manner of speaking." The blond gentleman smiled warmly. "Your father was cousin to Carlton Donaldson, as was my mother, though what that makes us, I vow I do not know. Suffice to say, we both appear on the family tree. I am Noel Donaldson Kemp."

"Ah, yes," Matthew said. Finally relaxing his cool gray scrutiny of the blond gentleman, he gave his attention to Sarah. "Miss Sterling," he said, "allow me to present Mr. Kemp. In paying me this visit, he has shown himself to be a gentleman of some fairmindedness, for you must know, he is the relative whose place I usurped as heir to Donmore Hall."

Chapter Four

Dinner was not as difficult as Sarah had at first supposed it might be, for Mr. Kemp was as socially adroit as he was handsome. "Having only just come from London yourself, Miss Sterling, you must have read all about the new heiress-apparent to the throne, a little girl born to the duke and Duchess of Kent."

"I have, sir. Victoria, I believe she is to be called. A pretty name."

"Quite. Though I believe Prinny was disappointed with the choice. Though his brother wished the child named for her mother, rumor has it the Prince Regent wished the child called Georgina, in compliment to himself."

Into this scintillating conversation their host tossed not one gambit, preferring to sit quietly at the head of the highly polished mahogany dinner table and glare down its length at his relative. Not that Sarah allowed his boorish manners to intrude upon her enjoyment of either the excellent food or the company of a personable young man. Instead, she smiled at Mr. Kemp and commented upon his good fortune in having visited Northumberland so often.

"This is marvelous country, sir, quite wild and beautiful, and I should not be at all surprised to discover that in the autumn the reds, golds, and oranges of the surrounding hills and vales are magnificent."

"Spoken like an artist," he said, smiling to show the

remark was meant as a compliment. "As you surmise, the autumn is rather pretty, but it is far too short. And believe me, it can get dashed cold in the north country once the snows come. With the onset of winter, I should not be at all surprised if you were considerably less enthusiastic about the area."

"Nay, sir. You cannot discourage me, for I like the cold. I find it invigorating. At least," she added, looking rather pointedly at Mr. Matthew Donaldson, "cold *weather* is invigorating. There is a coldness of another sort that one must always take in abhorrence."

There was a slight movement at the corners of her employer's mouth; otherwise Sarah saw no indication that her barb had found its mark.

"Miss Sterling," he said quietly, "have you your reticule with you?"

"No, sir, I have not."

"Unwise. I suggest, madam, that if you would challenge a larger, and I might add, a far from civilized opponent, that you wait until such time as you are in possession of an equalizer."

Sarah discovered within herself a desire to chuckle, and to resist that temptation, she looked away from her host, giving her attention to the wineglass she had not touched during the entire meal. Keeping her eyes downcast, she lifted the finely cut crystal to her lips for a minuscule sip of the Bordeaux.

After a minute or two of silence, Mr. Kemp reclaimed her attention. "I say, Miss Sterling, do you ride? There was used to be a rather pretty behaved mare in the stables that would do nicely for a lady. Perhaps—"

"Miss Sterling does not care for horseflesh."

Sarah nearly choked on the wine. When Matthew Donaldson had sat like a stone for most of the meal, contributing nothing, why had he chosen to serve up that piece of information? What he said was no more than the truth, of course, but his recalling it led her to a memory that sent the warmth rushing to her cheeks. As if it had happened only moments before, she fancied she could still feel him lifting her down from the stagecoach, holding her close against his broad chest, his muscular arms around her waist.

"Is aught amiss?" he asked, the devilish light in his eyes telling her that he had guessed her thoughts.

"No, sir," she replied with what calm she could command. "I was merely recalling how *very* unpleasant it can be to come face-to-face with an animal."

"Or eye to eye?" he suggested. "Up close, where the animal can smell the clean, fresh scent of your hair, or the—"

"Sir!" she said, turning quickly to Mr. Kemp, "I thank you for your suggestion regarding the mare, but it is as Mr. Donaldson said, I am not overly fond of horses."

"Then perhaps," the gentleman said, "we might go for a drive while the nice weather holds. I could show you a bit of the neighborhood. Especially those places I liked best when I visited here as a lad."

"You are very kind, but perhaps I should inform you that I am not a guest at Donmore Hall. I am here to do a job of work."

The gentleman blinked, as if unsure he had heard her correctly. "Work? I do not underst—"

"Miss Sterling is here to see to the cleaning of some of the paintings," Matthew Donaldson said.

Since he chose to say nothing of her other duties, Sarah rightly assumed that he did not want the visitor to know of her ability to assess the authenticity of the collection. Not that she would have discussed her work with anyone other than her employer.

Still, she had to wonder why Mr. Kemp could not know. For a time, at least, he had been the heir apparent to the Hall and to the collection. Surely Mr.

Matthew Donaldson could have no reason to suspect him of having anything to do with the missing inventory list or the possible substitution of copies for some of the originals.

Whatever his suspicions, Sarah admitted that they were none of her concern, and she vowed to keep her tongue between her teeth unless asked for her opinion. Having made that silent vow, she was suddenly obliged to cover an openmouthed yawn. Blushing at her lapse of manners, she pressed her napkin to her lips, set the linen beside her plate, and turned once again toward the head of the table.

"If you will excuse me, I shall leave you and your guest to your port."

While a footman hurried to hold her chair, both gentlemen stood.

Sarah executed a brief curtsy. "Good night, Mr. Kemp. Mr. Donaldson."

Mr. Kemp made as if to protest. "Good night? but surely, ma'am, you would not deprive us of the pleasure of your company in the drawing room?"

She shook her head. An exhausting morning of travel, coupled with the beginning of her employment, had all but done her in. "I beg you will forgive my rudeness, sir. Another evening, perhaps."

The footman was already opening the door for her when Matthew Donaldson spoke. "A word with you, if you please, Miss Sterling."

"Of course, sir."

Assuming he would speak with her there, Sarah paused, but to her surprise he slipped his hand beneath her elbow and led her from the room. They had arrived at the foot of the grand staircase before he addressed her again.

"You are discreet," he said, his voice just above a whisper, "that is good. Continue to be so. Trust no one."

Sarah felt those alarm bells go off in her head once again, and with them came a frisson of fear. To hide her uneasiness, she said, "I am to trust no one, sir? Not even you?"

He smiled, and it was the first genuine smile she had ever seen upon his face. It started with a light in his eyes, then it seemed to sneak up on his mouth, tugging at the corners until he relented, letting those sharply defined lips part to reveal white, even teeth.

"Madam," he said, "when I bade you trust no one, I meant especially not me."

Even though Sarah was in a strange bed, she had no trouble falling asleep. As tired as she was, she would have slept soundly on a meager cot in some stuffy attic room, but thankfully, such privation was far from her actual experience. Within minutes of her return to her lovely yellow bedchamber, she was tucked up in the large carved oak bed, with a thick feather mattress beneath her and a satin coverlet drawn up to her shoulders.

The day had been eventful enough to keep anyone awake, yet it did not do so. From the moment her head touched the pillow, Sarah did not stir, not until some time around seven the next morning when Morag tiptoed from the dressing room to the bedchamber door to let herself out of the room.

Servants in a large household rose early to partake of a breakfast presided over by the housekeeper, and aware of this practice, Sarah chose not to let the maid know she was awake. Actually, she did not want to break her fast at that time. Still stiff from her long journey, she yearned for some exercise before her workday began. Deciding that a walk in the fresh air was just what she needed, and remembering how pretty the area was to the south, beyond the stables, Sarah settled upon that as her destination.

She made quick work of her ablutions, then she dressed for a turn out-of-doors, lacing up her walking boots and donning a mantle of French gray superfine trimmed in gold braid. After fastening the hip-length cape at the neck, and checking to be certain she had a handkerchief in the lining pocket, she made her way to the staircase. Though she met no one in the corridor, at the bottom of the stairs she heard the clink of dishes and the voices of a pair of maids who were setting up a buffet in the small room next to the dining room.

If nothing else, I have discovered where breakfast is served.

Sarah breathed deeply, recognizing the unmistakable aroma of grilled kippers, as well as the fragrance of rich, freshly brewed coffee. The very thought of kippers made her mouth water, but she was resolved to stretch her muscles before giving in to the temptations that beckoned to her empty stomach. That resolution in mind, she hurried down the corridor to the back of the house and let herself out the rear door.

The moment she stepped outside, she realized that a walk of any kind was out of the question. The world seemed to be enfolded in an impenetrable fog, and visibility was limited to that area within her arm's reach. Her father had warned her about the perils of northern summer weather, having once been lost for hours on a mountain in Scotland when an unexpected mist rolled in from the sea. The warning notwithstanding, Sarah had not been prepared for such denseness.

It was as though she were alone in the world, and even those few sounds that penetrated the thickness took on a distorted, almost otherworldly quality. Pure foolishness, of course. Mist and fog were perfectly natural. They had something to do with cold air flowing down the hillsides during the night and accumulating at the valley bottom. As the air warmed after dawn, it rose and mixed with the cooler air, forming fog or low clouds. Nothing otherworldly there.

Furthermore, the house was just behind her, and it was filled with people. If she was too nervous to continue, she had only to take a step back and open the door. Besides, what had she to be nervous about? This was not Scotland, nor was she mountain climbing. Still, she was torn, for though she did not wish to give in to foolish fancy, she could ill afford to take reckless chances.

The solution, when it came to her, was so logical Sarah wondered why she had not thought of it sooner. She could have her walk in the fresh air, all she need do was circle the house, keeping the red Cumbrian sandstone of the walls always within sight. Happy with this decision, she pulled the hood of her mantle up over her head to shield her from the unexpected coolness of the damp air, tied the drawstrings beneath her chin, then began her walk.

All went well for the first ten minutes. Since the ground was fairly level, she strolled along at a pretty good pace, passing the east wing and turning left to continue past the front of the house, occasionally checking to assure herself that the sandstone walls were still in view. Unfortunately, she had not taken into consideration the fact that she had never seen the lay of the land beside the west wing.

As she turned the corner, what had once been solid ground beneath her feet was suddenly nothing but empty space. She pitched forward into that space, and for several heart-stopping seconds she tumbled down a grassy slope. When she feared she might continue to roll forever, perhaps until she plunged headlong down the side of a mountain, she came to an abrupt stop, her right shoulder colliding with the base of a large oak tree whose long, spreading limbs stretched almost to the ground.

Though her shoulder cried out at the harsh treatment, Sarah was more frightened than injured, and for
a minute or so she lay very still, clutching that wonderfully solid tree and gasping for breath. In time,
when her breathing slowed to something resembling
its normal pace, and her heart slid from her throat
back down to her chest, she sat up, hoping to regain
her bearings.

She looked about her, straining to see something—
anything—through the copious, tapering leaves, but
all she saw were more leaves and the mist beyond. It
was while she sat there, trying to decide what was best
to do, that she heard the voices. They were muffled,
eerie voices that seemed to float toward her through
the thick mist.

"Stubble it!" said the first one.

It was a man speaking, and his dialect was that of a
Cockney from the East End of London.

"I'd as soon slit your gullet as not," he said. "I could
do it right 'ere, right now, and there'd be none to care
and none the wiser."

He made a guttural sound that was probably meant
to simulate a throat being cut, and Sarah's stomach
threatened to surrender last evening's meal.

Another voice, this one so indistinct she could not
determine if it belonged to man or maid, said something Sarah could not make out.

"Shut your yap!" the Cockney ordered. "You're a
sniveling coward, you are, and worthless into the bargain."

The other voice said something else, but that, too,
was unintelligible.

"But you 'aven't brought it like you promised, now
'ave you. All we've 'ad is your fine talk."

There was silence for a time, silence broken by a sort
of yelp, like someone or something crying out from a
blow.

"Mr. Wayford wants wot was promised 'im, and if you know wot's good for you, you'll not keep 'im waiting. Not a patient man is Mr. Wayford."

Another muffled cry.

"You got a fortnight. No more. If you b'ain't in Lunnon by then, with the promised goods, I'll be back. And the day I come back, that'll be your last day this side of hell."

As suddenly as the voices had come, they drifted away. In the quiet that followed, Sarah heard nothing save her own breathing, and the silence was almost as frightening as what she had overheard.

She could think of only one thing, getting away from there without being discovered by the man who had issued the threats. Hoping the mist might have dissipated somewhat, offering her a glimpse of the sandstone walls of the Hall, she pushed herself onto her hands and knees and began to feel her way out from under the low-lying limbs of the oak, moving as quietly and quickly as possible.

Her sodden clothing made movement doubly difficult. As if to punish her for being so foolish as to come out-of-doors in the first place, her skirts insisted upon wrapping around her legs and bunching between her knees, making every inch of ground covered seem more like a mile. Despite the wet clothes, and the fact that she could see nothing beyond the tree limbs, Sarah was at least encouraged by the tilt of the land, for she was definitely headed uphill.

Once she was free of the branches, she peeled her clinging skirts away from her shaking legs and stumbled to her feet. Upright at last, she was about to take her first tenuous step when she realized she was not alone.

Before she could draw breath to scream, a hand reached out from behind her and clamped over her mouth. At the same time, a powerful arm caught her around the waist and pulled her flush against a hard, unyielding body.

"Shh," he whispered into her ear. "Be very still, and do not make a sound."

Even before she heard his voice, Sarah knew who held her. It was Matthew Donaldson. Perhaps she recognized his touch, after all, he had held her before, or maybe some sixth sense had told her that he was near. Whatever the reason, she did not struggle. Instead, she leaned against his reassuringly solid chest, and though the buttons of his waistcoat pressed into her cheek, she was much too glad of his support to complain of discomfort or care that it was totally improper for her not to try to move away.

They stood thus for a full minute, his arm holding her immobile, his hand still over her mouth, and while Matthew listened for further sounds in the cloaking mist, Sarah listened to his heart beat against her ear. The beat was steady, and so calm that she wondered if he had heard the whole of that furtive conversation.

In time he relaxed the hand that covered her mouth, but before he released her completely, he bent his head and whispered in her ear once again. "We are going back to the house. Say nothing until we are inside."

She nodded her assent, far too happy to be in the company of a reliable guide to argue at his rather peremptory instructions.

Holding tightly to his hand, she let him lead her where he would, and within a very short time she felt cobblestones beneath her boots. She breathed a sigh of relief, recognizing the path that ran from the stables to the steward's office and the book room.

Her rescuer chose to ignore the office door, continuing instead to the French windows, which he opened quietly. After stepping inside the book room, he yanked her none too gently after him, then he closed the windows and turned the key in the lock.

The only light in the room came from the fire that burned brightly beneath the marble mantelpiece, but after the cold, impenetrable grayness of the out-of-doors, the yellow radiance seemed bright as the sun. Other than warming the room, the flames gave enough illumination to show the mist that clung in shiny droplets to Matthew Donaldson's dark hair. Unfortunately, they also gave enough light to reveal the muscle that twitched angrily in his angular jaw.

"And now," he said, the softly spoken words at odds with that angry twitch, "would you care to tell me what the deuce you were doing outside?"

Sarah knew he had every right to be displeased with her, for she had been foolish and she knew it. But hers was an independent nature—*bullheaded* was her father's term for it—and she had never taken kindly to being asked to explain her actions. "I should think what I was doing was obvious."

"It is not obvious to me. Otherwise, I would not have asked the question."

Remembering that this man was her employer, Sarah willed herself to speak evenly. "I was taking a walk. Not that I can think why you would be interested in my activities. Especially not in light of what you must have overheard. That man—"

"You were taking a walk," he repeated, as though she had said nothing else. "In this mist?"

"Since you found me outside, sir, I can only assume your question is rhetorical."

That muscle in his jaw twitched again, and this time the tone of his voice was decidedly sharp. "Did no one warn you of the danger of such an excursion? Even when one is familiar with the area—which you are not!—going abroad in such weather is foolish beyond permission. I would have expected a woman of your intelligence to have more sense."

This was beginning to sound like a scolding, and

Sarah did like it one bit. She was wet. She was cold.
And the shoulder that had collided with the trunk of
the oak tree was beginning to throb as though it had a
life of its own. "And I would have expected a man
with a fortune in art to be more interested in guarding
his paintings than in berating a person who made an
understandable error in judgment."

"Madam, I can purchase more paintings. A human
life is not so easily replaced."

"A human life? But, surely I was never in any real
danger."

He did not reply to her surmise, merely raised one
sardonic eyebrow as if to let that gesture speak for
him. As he looked at her, Sarah recalled how frightened she had been when she fell—frightened that she
might be closer than she knew to the edge of some
precipice. She recalled as well how grateful she had
been to feel Matthew Donaldson's arm around her, to
feel his solid, reassuring body supporting hers.

Never one to deny the truth, no matter how badly it
reflected upon her, she was forced to acknowledge the
justice of what he had said. "You are right, of course,
sir. I was foolish to go outside in such weather. But rest
assured, I will not do so again. I try never to make the
same mistake twice."

"A philosophy to live by," he said.

He was quiet for a time, and though his face revealed none of his thoughts, something very like regret showed in his eyes. "I suggest, Miss Sterling, that
you return to your room while I ring for Bailey. He
will see to sending up some hot water, enough for a
hip bath. A good soak will relieve any stiffness resulting from your fall."

A tub filled with steaming water sounded like
heaven to Sarah, and she was already imagining herself luxuriating in the warmth when it penetrated her
brain that her employer was still talking.

"By the time you have had your bath and a meal," he said, "the fog should be lifted. Have the maid pack your clothes, and I will have someone drive you to the village."

"Pack my clothes? But, I—"

"I believe it would be wisest for all concerned if you returned to London on the next stage."

The iciness of her clammy clothing was nothing compared to the cold that invaded Sarah's bones at his pronouncement. "But, sir. I have assured you that I will exercise the greatest of caution from now on. Furthermore, I thought you needed that inventory immediately."

Clutching at this straw to save her from being dismissed, she said, "You did hear the voices, did you not?"

"I heard."

Thank heaven! At least she would not be obliged to convince him of that chilling conversation. "I cannot be certain, of course, but I believe the 'promised goods' the man threatened the other person about are the paintings. Your paintings."

Her employer's face registered not the least surprise. When he said nothing, and merely ran his hands through his crisp hair to dislodge the droplets that still clung there, Sarah continued. "The man seemed quite angry. And dangerous."

"Very dangerous. Which is why I want you away from here."

"But, sir, I—"

"Today."

The single word was spoken with such finality that Sarah could think of no argument to dissuade him from turning her out. Thus, while he rang for the butler, she turned and walked to the door. Her hand was already on the handle when she recalled something else the voice in the mist had said—something that just might gain her a reprieve.

"Sir," she said, her shoulders squared almost defiantly, "I cannot go today."

"Madam, you can, and you will."

Afraid her nerve might desert her if she gave it half a chance, Sarah spoke quickly. "But you heard what that man said. He gave the person to whom he spoke a fortnight to bring the goods to London. *London*," she repeated for emphasis. "For all we know, the man—an individual you agreed is dangerous—may be waiting at the inn this very minute to board the stage you would put me on."

She gave Matthew a moment to reply, and when he did not do so, and merely stared at her, in his eyes a mixture of anger and concern, she played her trump card. "I may have acted imprudently in going abroad in the mist, sir, but I am not so foolish as to willingly share a coach with a person who has threatened to slit another person's gullet."

"Damnation," Matthew muttered.

Feeling that she had said enough, she quit the room. Though she moved with more speed than usual, she was not quick enough to avoid hearing her employer's final decree.

"Tomorrow, then," he said. "And believe me, madam, you *will* leave. Even if I have to toss you over my shoulder and put you on the coach by main force."

Chapter Five

Nevertheless, Sarah did not leave Donmore Hall the next day, thanks in part to a giant oak tree whose timely uprooting blocked the road south, bringing all coach travel in that direction to a standstill. This unexpected news was delivered by an equally unexpected visitor, a Lady Worthing, cousin to the late Carlton Donaldson.

"We might have been killed," Lady Worthing declared the moment Bailey assisted her from her maroon traveling chaise.

Obviously well acquainted with the Donmore butler, she began immediately to regale the servant with an account of their narrow escape. "But for John Coachman's quick thinking in putting the whip to the team the moment he heard that awful creaking noise, we might even now be crushed beneath those deadly branches."

Bailey gasped. "Your ladyship! Are you injured? May I offer you my arm?"

Though Bailey was duly shocked, it was obvious to Sarah, who had hurried to the gallery window at the first sound of carriage wheels crunching upon the gravel carriageway, that the tall, bony woman was more excited than frightened.

After the visitor had adjusted the swansdown tippet that perfectly matched her pomona green pelisse and carriage dress, and had given a tug to the ruched silk bonnet whose narrow poke revealed steel gray curls resting against thin, rouged cheeks, she placed her hand on the butler's arm as if conveying upon him a royal favor. However, before she allowed him to lead her toward the massive double doors and into the fieldstone vestibule, she instructed him to see her coachman was rewarded with a glass of Mr. Donaldson's best brandy.

"And you might bring a glass of sherry to my room, for my nerves are quite overset."

"If it please your ladyship, I will bring the refreshments to the drawing room. The housekeeper will need a few minutes to see a bedchamber is made ready for you."

"The drawing room it is, then. That is, if your new master keeps a fire lit there on these cool days."

"He does, ma'am."

"Very good. See my things are taken up to the yellow bedchamber as soon as it is made ready. My maid can inform the housekeeper of those little extras I will require. As for my niece, I suggest she be given the small chamber at the top of the stairs. I am persuaded she will not wish to be situated too great a distance from me."

Sparing a moment to glance back over her shoulder, Lady Worthing called to a young woman who was being handed down from the coach by a besotted-looking postilion. "Come along, Chloe."

"Yes, Aunt Agatha," replied the soft-spoken damsel.

No more than the lad was Sarah able to take her eyes from the vision—a breathtaking creature in palest pink twilled silk—for she was the most beautiful girl Sarah had ever seen. Elegantly slender, she was a delicate wisp of a girl, and the very antithesis of the raw-boned Lady Worthing. A disinterested party might be forgiven for wondering how two such dissimilar females could be related.

It was Bailey who reclaimed Sarah's attention with a discreet cough. "Your pardon, my lady, but the yellow bedchamber is not available."

"Not available? What nonsense is this? There was nothing wrong with it when I stayed here last."

"Nor is there now, my lady. It is just that Miss Sterling is occupying the chamber at the moment."

Her ladyship's voice was edged with icy disbelief. "Miss Sterling? I know no such person. Who is she, and what is she doing here?" Then, with a gasp, "Never tell me that Donaldson is already betrothed!"

While Bailey stammered some sort of reply, Sarah heard an oath muttered just behind her.

"Damnation!" Matthew Donaldson said.

Sarah jumped back as though she had been caught with her hand in the church poor box. Though, truth be told, she might have preferred that to being caught eavesdropping. "Sir, I did not know you were—"

"Shh," he said, stepping to the side of the window and peeping down at the chaise. Speaking very softly so they could not be overheard from the carriageway, he asked, "Who the blazes is down there?"

Embarrassed to admit that she had been listening long enough to know the person's identity, Sarah dissembled. "I am sure I cannot say."

"Devil take it, woman, do not turn missish on me. Not now."

Sarah was tempted to tell him that she did not appreciate being sworn at and to advise him to mind his tongue. Instead, she replied with cloying sweetness, "Whoever the visitors may be, they have brought news of the road south. It is closed to coach traffic, impassable for a time. The result of a fallen tree."

Ignoring the visitors for the moment, her employer stepped away from the window, stopping mere inches from her. His eyes were like flints, and though his voice was still just above a whisper, his words were emphatic. "I wanted you away from Donmore Hall today. In fact, I came here for no other purpose than to assure myself that you were packed and ready to be put safely aboard the London-bound stage."

Since he stood quite close to her, Sarah was obliged to tilt her head back to look up at him. Disciplining her features into what she hoped was a guileless expression, she said, "It would seem that nature has other plans."

Matthew looked into her upturned face and fought the urge to laugh, not deceived for an instant by that conveniently donned mask of meekness. Miss Sarah Sterling had nerve, he would give her that, but if she only knew it, those honest brown eyes of hers gave her away. She wanted to remain here to complete the inventory and restoration of the art collection, and all the while she lifted that pseudo-innocent face toward him, her eyes confirmed that she was secretly thanking nature for intervening on her behalf.

Hoping to convince her of his very real concern for her safety, he placed his hands on her shoulders so that she would give him her full attention. "Yesterday you asked me if I had heard those voices in the mist. It was while I stood there, listening to the man's threats, that I realized the danger I had put you in."

"Me? I see no reason why anyone should wish me harm."

"Madam, you are very naive."

His fingers tightened, all but biting into her flesh. "Believe me, whoever has designs upon the paintings in this room—and it could be any of several suspects— he, or she, is mixed up with some nasty characters. I am not unacquainted with the type. Having spent six years of my army career as a soldier of the line, I came into contact with more than one felon who joined up to keep from being hanged or transported. To a man, those blackguards would slit a person's throat for a few quid."

A moment's hesitation showed in her eyes, and he knew she was recalling the thug's own words. Pressing his advantage, he continued. "Who can say what such men would do if they believed they could get their hands on paintings worth thousands of pounds? Or what they would do to anyone who got in their way?"

"I . . . I take your meaning, sir, and I apologize for not having thought the matter through. You must, of course, safeguard your property, and you cannot do that if you are obliged to guard me as well." She lowered her gaze, but not before Matthew saw the regret in her eyes. "I will be ready to leave as soon as the road is cleared."

Matthew loosened his grip on her shoulders. This was all his fault, of course. When she had first arrived at the Hall, he should have followed his better judgment and sent her away that very moment. He should have paid her the promised amount for the job and put her on the next stage. And he would have done so if she had not drawn that ridiculous pistol, making him laugh for the first time in months.

He had allowed himself to be diverted by her spirit, and that was his first mistake.

A scratching at the gallery door intruded upon Matthew's memory of Sarah brandishing the firearm, and though he stepped away from her before calling permission for the applicant to enter, he fancied he could still feel the softness of her shoulders. To his dismay, their warmth seemed imprinted upon his palms.

Bailey stopped just inside the doorway. "Lady Worthing has arrived, sir. Accompanied by her niece. I took the liberty of showing her ladyship and the young lady to the drawing room."

The young lady! Damnation! Had the matchmaking

mamas abandoned propriety completely? Was a man not safe from their machinations even in his own home?

"Who the deuce is this woman? I do not recall any Worthings in the neighborhood."

The butler cleared his throat discreetly. "Her ladyship is not from Northumberland, sir, but from Sussex. She is a member of the family, being a first cousin to Mr. Carlton Donaldson. In years past, she and Sir William often visited at the Hall."

"And the niece?" Matthew asked. "Did she usually accompany Sir William and Lady Worthing on those previous trips north?"

"No, sir. This is the young lady's first visit."

"Somehow," Matthew said, his tone sarcastic, "I suspected it might be."

Sarah watched this exchange in silence. It was obvious from her employer's questions that he was not pleased with this unexpected visit. In this instance, however, she doubted that his displeasure had anything to do with art thieves. Judging by his sarcasm, and her own knowledge of the world, the society matrons must be presenting their daughters to his notice at every turn. It was a given that once the news spread that a single gentleman had just inherited a handsome estate and a fortune in art, the mamas would not rest until they ran the poor fellow to the ground like a fox during hunting season.

"Tell Lady Worthing I will join her directly."

"I will inform her, sir."

When the butler did not quit the room immediately, Matthew Donaldson asked him if there was something else.

Bailey did not look at his employer, but concentrated his attention on the deal worktable and the braided leather chair that stood beside it. "Upon her ladyship's previous visits, sir, she stayed in the west wing, occupying the yellow bedchamber. She holds a certain fondness for that apartment, and since I chanced to overhear Morag mention that Miss Sterling was leaving today, I wondered if perhaps the bedchamber might be available for—"

"You may put Lady Worthing in the west wing. I am persuaded she will find the blue bedchamber every bit as comfortable as the yellow. As for Miss Sterling, her plans have changed. Now that there are ladies in the house, she has agreed to remain as long as they do."

Once the butler bowed himself out and closed the door behind him, Matthew turned to the lady whose comings and goings he had mandated with such a cavalier disregard for her own preferences. From the way she was looking at him, hope shining from those soft brown eyes, she was not displeased with the outcome.

"I want it understood," he said, "that the minute the visitors leave, so do you."

"Understood."

"And one more thing."

"Yes, sir?"

"Under no circumstances are you to leave the Hall alone."

Even before she spoke, he knew she was about to object to his terms. He had given enough orders in his lifetime to know when unquestioned obedience went against a person's nature, and from the slight pursing of her soft lips, he could see that submission did not come easily for her. Not that he faulted her for it. A person had to learn to stand up for herself, especially a young woman obliged to earn her own living.

"Surely a walk on the grounds would not—"

"Especially not a walk on the grounds! Have you forgotten what happened last time?"

The question had been innocent enough, yet it brought a sudden rosy hue to her cheeks, color totally unwarranted by the recollection of being lost in the mist.

"What is this?" he asked. "What did I say to put you to the blush?"

Her color deepened, and though unaware of its cause, Matthew reached out and brushed his thumb across her cheek, as if to erase the stain. That was his second mistake.

The moment he touched her satiny skin, that lustful animal he had joked about came to life. Unfortunately, the joke was on Matthew, for as he stood there, so close to her he could smell the faint hint of lavender that seemed to come from her warmed skin, all he could think of was his desire to slip his hand around to the nape of her neck and draw her to him for a kiss.

Luckily, he remembered just in time that Sarah Sterling was not some willing tavern wench, but a lady unaccustomed to the rough manners of a soldier. Not that he would have treated her roughly, of course; that was not his way. He liked his women willing.

His women! Heaven help him, where had that notion come from?

Realizing that his thoughts were getting out of hand, he decided his wisest course would be to make a strategic retreat before he did or said something he would regret. With this object in mind, he stepped back, made her a brief bow, and quit the room.

Only after the door had closed behind him did Sarah remember to breathe. She filled her lungs, for they were completely empty. When Matthew Donaldson had brushed his thumb across her cheek, sending a flood of warmth down her spine, her lungs had apparently forgotten how to function.

In and out. In and out. Far wiser to concentrate on the rhythm of her breathing than on the wild beating of her heart.

He had wanted to kiss her. Even a female with little

experience of the opposite sex knew that look in a man's eyes. Not that she took it as a sign of any serious attraction on his part. After all, he had warned her how it might be. The day she had arrived at the Hall, he had informed her that he was no gentleman, and that having a female in his home day after day might bring out the animal lusts within him.

At the time, she had thought he was merely trying to frighten her into leaving, but apparently that was not the case. Of course, after today there was little chance that he would ever want to kiss her again; just as there was little chance of his holding her close against him as he had done when he found her on the grounds, lost in the mist. Today the beautiful Miss Worthing had arrived, and once Matthew Donaldson beheld that ravishing creature, the animal within him would very likely forget that Sarah was even in the house.

Strangely, that thought, far from consoling her, left her feeling unaccountably melancholy.

"Lady Worthing," Matthew said, bowing to the hook-nosed female who had disposed herself upon the rose brocade settee as though she were a queen and the settee a throne. Not a handsome woman, she was on the wrong side of sixty, with gray hair and faded blue eyes, and like many of her contemporaries, her face was powdered and rouged, and she wore a small heart-shaped patch to the left of her mouth.

"Donaldson," she said, offering her hand for his kiss. "I thought it only proper that I call, for I am one who believes that every attention should be paid the head of one's family."

Matthew approached the lady, took her proffered hand, and lifted the mittened knuckles to his lips for the briefest of salutes. "Very solicitous of you, ma'am, but to tell the truth, I had not thought there was any family to head. When my father died, I got the distinct impression that I was alone in the world."

For a moment, the woman looked decidedly ill at ease, but she recouped by informing Matthew that his father had always been a favorite with her. "For you must know," she said, her hand to her heart, "that I am as foolish as the next woman when it comes to a handsome rogue. And Cousin George was nothing if not handsome."

"And nothing," Matthew added, "if not a rogue. Did he leave this mortal coil owing you money, ma'am?"

Her ladyship's upper lip twitched, as if she had caught a whiff of some unpleasant odor, and her host waited patiently to see if she would choose to be offended and give him a setdown. She did not, and the fact that she smiled at him before continuing with her reminiscences made Matthew decidedly uneasy. If the old grandam was willing to endure such insolence, she must be quite eager to make a match of it between him and her niece.

And now that he thought of it, where was the fiancée elect?

Matthew had not spied the young woman when he entered the drawing room. Was she hidden in some shadowed corner? Was she so unhandsome her relative had thought it best for her not to be exposed to the revealing light?

This unworthy thought had no sooner occurred to him than Lady Worthing blessed herself for a ninnyhammer. "Here am I chattering on about my own side of the family and completely forgetting my husband's niece. Donaldson, pray allow me to make you known to Miss Chloe Worthing."

"How do you do?" came a soft voice from the far corner of the room.

Matthew turned to find a dainty vision in pink

standing beside the pianoforte, a piece of sheet music in her hands. "Forgive me, sir," said the dark-haired beauty, "I hope you do not mind my looking through your music?"

"Not at all," he replied, making her a bow. "May *I* hope that you will favor us with a few selections after dinner?"

A faint blush tinted the ivory skin, and the young lady lowered her unbelievably long lashes, shielding her large blue eyes from view. "I should be happy to play for you, sir, if that is your wish. Though I promise you, I am not at all proficient."

Not proficient? As if anyone would notice. When a chit possessed such unparalleled beauty, gentlemen seldom cared if she was accomplished, or even sensible. For most men, it would be enough merely to be allowed to gaze at the perfection of Miss Chloe Worthing's face and form.

Upon those thoughts intruded the voice of Mr. Noel Kemp, who chose that moment to enter the room. "Cousin," he said, still exuding the unshakable cheerfulness he had exhibited for the two days of his residence. "I was told you were in here, and I wished to know if you played billiards. I have examined the table, and it is in good condition. If you should not dislike it, after dinner we could—"

He paused, his mouth agape as he beheld the lady by the piano. "Chloe?" he said, disbelief evident in his tone.

The young lady blushed to the roots of her dusky curls. "Hello, Noel."

"Kemp!" Lady Worthing interjected in tones so sharp they made the young gentleman jump. "Pray heaven, what are you doing here? When Cousin Carlton banished you from the premises, I thought you were denied the hospitality of Donmore Hall forever."

Something very like anger showed on Noel Kemp's

handsome face, though when he spoke, his manner was as even-tempered as ever. *"Banished* is a harsh word, Cousin Agatha, for something that was no more than a misunderstanding. Moreover, it was a misunderstanding that could have been cleared up in a trice had time permitted. Unfortunately, the old gentleman received his notice to quit before our reconciliation could be accomplished."

While the foursome drank tea in the drawing room, Sarah got on with her work in the gallery. Because she had expected to leave the Hall that very day, she had worked diligently yesterday afternoon and this morning to finish the inventory Matthew Donaldson needed. She was examining the final painting, a richly textured portrait of a young boatman in a blue, tasseled cap, when Angus Newsome entered the gallery.

Though quite certain from the arrangement of color, and the relationship of mass and space, that the work had, indeed, been executed by the Flemish artist, Hans Eworth, Sarah did not add her findings to the inventory at that time. Instead she chose to cover the topmost page with a blank piece of paper. She would wait until she was alone to make her notations concerning the painting.

"Good day, to you, miss," the steward said.

Sarah had not seen the man since her arrival at Donmore, when he had warned her not to remain, that the Hall was no fit place for a decent woman. All things considered, he looked remarkably better than he had that day.

His left eye, which had been all but swollen shut, appeared more normal, and the skin around the eye, which had been a bright black and blue, now sported a dull yellowish overtone. His bottom lip had improved as well, and the split in the corner seemed to be healing nicely. As for the angry bruise on his chin, that, too, was much less noticeable.

Since to remark on an obvious beating would be the height of rudeness, she pretended not to notice, asking him instead if he had come to the gallery for some particular reason.

"Nothing specific, miss."

His words lacked the ring of truth. Something about the man, perhaps it was the unfortunate condition of his face, made Sarah uneasy. Or it could be nothing more than the memory of their first meeting, when he had done nothing to hide his bias against her.

"I just wanted to see how you were getting on," he said. "On account of my not living at the Hall proper, but down at the gatehouse, we've not seen each other, so I thought I'd come up to see if you needed anything to help you in your work."

The words sounded genuine enough. Still, Sarah felt that if she should need help, the steward would be the last person she would consider asking. "I require nothing, but thank you for inquiring."

Because she chose not to discuss any part of her work with him, she attempted to turn the conversation by showing him her dirty hands. "Though I suppose you could be forgiven for thinking me in need of a basin of water and a bar of strong soap."

Newsome smiled, but if there was any sincerity in the gesture, it did not show in his eyes. Instead, he looked rather pointedly at the depiction of the young boatman in the blue cap.

"Nice painting," he said.

"You appreciate art, do you, Mr. Newsome?"

"I know aught of such things," he replied, "but a working man can appreciate a bit of color same as a gentleman."

Sarah had no idea how she should answer that slightly belligerent remark, and to her relief, the stew-

ard began to walk the length of the room, gazing at the
works displayed on the long wall, his hands stuffed
into the pockets of his serviceable gray coat. When he
stopped before a small, gilt-framed painting of two
children, their sashes almost as pink as the scalp that
showed beneath his carefully combed hair, he turned
and asked Sarah the name of the artist.

"I cannot say, Mr. Newsome."

His dull green eyes narrowed. "Cannot or will not?"

Thankfully, she was not obliged to answer his question, for Morag chose that moment to bring her a tray
bearing a pot of tea, a plate of sandwiches, and two
currant buns still hot from the oven.

"The house is at sixes and sevens," the maid said,
clearing a place on the corner of the deal table for the
tray, "on account of the visitors arriving unexpected
like. And with her ladyship's puffed-up maid giving
orders right and left like she was lady-in-waiting to
the Queen herself, I thought I'd play least in sight and
bring your nuncheon to you."

While the earnest-faced girl busied herself pouring
hot, fragrant bohea into a pretty rose-patterned China
cup, talking nonstop about the beautiful dresses the
young lady had brought with her from London,
Angus Newsome touched his finger to his forehead in
salute and left the gallery. Not that Sarah was sorry to
see him go. His presence had made her uncomfortable,
and she determined to ask Matthew Donaldson when
next she saw him, if there was a key to the gallery
door.

Chapter Six

As it transpired, Sarah forgot to ask for the key. Uppermost in her mind was the desire to put the inventory directly into Matthew Donaldson's hands, so the moment she finished the rather detailed list, she gathered up the numbered grid and the dozen or so pages, and without bothering to remove her dust-smudged apron, she hurried toward the main staircase.

Halfway down the carpeted stairs, she came face-to-face with Lady Worthing, who took instant exception to sharing that route with a person in an apron.

"What is this?" she asked, giving Sarah a look haughty enough to freeze a duke in his tracks. "Has discipline at Donmore Hall sunk to such a low the servants no longer use the back stairs?"

Though Sarah felt the heat of embarrassment travel up her neck to burn in her face, she spoke with as much dignity as she could muster. "I fear you have misunderstood the matter, ma'am, I am not—"

"*Lady Worthing* to you, my girl!"

While her scrawny bosom heaved with indignation, her ladyship stared meaningfully at Sarah's hair. "And where, pray, is your cap? I insist you cover your head, for if there is one thing I cannot tolerate in a servant, it is red hair."

"I should rather have called it brown," Matthew Donaldson said from the bottom of the stairs.

Both women jumped at his sudden appearance.

"Or more accurately," he continued, the words drawled and purposefully provocative, "brown burnished to a lustrous mahogany hue."

That the light of mischief flickered in those gray eyes did not escape Sarah's notice; nor, so it would appear, was it lost on her ladyship. The affronted lady gave Sarah a quick inspection from head to toe, then she returned her attention to Matthew.

"Donaldson," she said, her tone frosty as a winter's morning, "this will not do. Have you given no thought to what is owed your name?"

"Why, no," he replied, resting his forearm on the carved newel and propping one booted foot upon the bottom stair. "Should I have?"

Lady Worthing drew herself up stiffly, apparently affronted as much by Matthew's casual stance as by his words. "It grieves me deeply," she said, "that such a one should be heir to all this. Though I should have suspected how it would be, considering the life you chose. I had heard that you had a taste for low company, fraternizing with common soldiers and who knows what else besides, but I had hoped that some sign of your breeding might still be evident."

"That was your hope, was it, ma'am?" If anything, his drawl was more pronounced. "Somehow, I had surmised that you came to Northumberland cherishing another hope entirely."

"Sir," said the outraged lady, "you have the manners of a cur."

"See there," he said, looking up at Sarah, "did I not tell you that I was no gentleman?"

"Mr. Donaldson," Sarah said, hoping to put an end to his goading of the visitor, "I have those papers you wanted regarding the paintings in the gallery. With your approval, I can begin immediately with the restoration needed."

"Restoration?" her ladyship asked of her relative, ignoring Sarah as though she were no longer present. "What is she saying? Surely you have not been so foolish as to allow one of your . . . that *person* near the Donaldson collection."

He straightened, all humor gone from his eyes. "Miss Sterling came to me highly recommended."

"Of that," her ladyship said, her tone contemptuous, "I have no doubt."

His reply was deceptively quiet. "Hastily drawn conclusions, Lady Worthing, sometimes say more of the character of the judge than the one being judged."

An uncomfortable silence followed this remark, and only after her ladyship had adjusted the wrist button on her glove did she speak. "The collection is yours, Donaldson, and legally you may do with it what you will. However, I should be remiss in what I believe to be my duty to the family, if I did not tell you that to allow this young woman access to a fortune in art is unconscionable. As for giving her permission to attempt something so delicate as a restoration, I shudder to think of the possible damage. What can she know of such work?"

"Why do you not ask her yourself? The lady has a more than adequate command of the English language."

Sarah did not wait for the question. "I have letters of recommendation, ma'am, if you should wish to see them. Perhaps you have heard of my father, Mr. Garrick Sterling?"

"I have not," she replied, though she spoke with less hostility. "Your father is here with you, then, doing the actual restoration?"

"No, ma'am. He is at our home in London recuperating from a heart attack. I came to Donmore Hall to fulfill the contract he made with Mr. Donaldson."

"So you are here alone. Unchaperoned." She pursed

her mouth in disapproval. "You had much better have stayed in London, young woman, to nurse your father. 'Tis a far more fitting occupation for a female. And one, I might add, that would do you more credit."

The facade of meekness Sarah donned in the interest of maintaining employment was beginning to crack, and she had taken just about all the rudeness she could tolerate. "I assure you, ma'am, that my father is being cared for. It was more important to him, and to me, that I complete this commission."

With that she stepped around Lady Worthing and continued down the stairs, stopping only when she was beside her employer. "Shall we go into your book room, sir?"

Matthew moved aside to let her pass. "After you, Miss Sterling."

They had taken only a few steps when Lady Worthing sought to reclaim her host's attention. "Donaldson," she said, her tone once again conciliatory, "my niece is desirous of seeing the estate, and I assured her that you would be happy to show her about this afternoon."

Matthew executed a courtly bow. "You are correct, ma'am, I should be delighted to show Miss Worthing about the grounds, had I not already promised to escort Miss Sterling to the stables. She has been so busy since her arrival, that she has had no opportunity to visit the horses. And you must know, she is inordinately fond of horseflesh."

They did not, of course, visit the horses. Without batting an eye, Matthew Donaldson led the supposed equine lover past the neat tile-roofed stables, then preceded her onto a narrow path that wound gently downward toward the valley. Not that Sarah offered any objections to the change in plan; she was far too

happy to be out-of-doors to find fault with any destination.

Nor could this particular route be faulted. To the
contrary, for the view was breathtaking. The path had
been formed by countless decades of feet, and worn so
smooth it was possible for a person to ramble along at
a good pace while still giving their full attention to the
rugged beauty of the distant hills and vales.

"Does the scenery meet with your approval,
madam?"

"I should be hard to please, sir, if it did not."

If the truth were known, Sarah had not expected
such an outing. Though she had said nothing at the
time, she believed her employer's invented excuse for
not escorting the lovely Miss Worthing about the estate was but a tale told to annoy the lady's aunt. Thus,
Sarah had been surprised when he took the inventory
from her, locked the sheets in the top drawer of his
desk, then told her to fetch her wrap.

"But, sir, I—"

"And the sturdiest boots you possess," he added,
"for if you can find it in your heart to forgo the
promised treat of visiting the horses, there is something I should like to show you."

"What is that, sir?"

He hesitated the merest second. "Another masterpiece."

A quarter of an hour later, adequately booted and
wearing the mantle she had worn the morning before
when she had taken her ill-fated walk in the mist,
Sarah followed Matthew Donaldson's lead down the
footpath. Though the sun shone brightly, the air was
slightly crisp—just the way she liked it—and the exercise was invigorating. With each step, Sarah felt her
spirits lifting.

For some time they meandered through a spruce
forest whose sharp, clean aroma filled the midsummer

air, but after about a mile, the path continued downward toward the village, while the hikers veered to the
right, making use of a barely discernible trail. Gradu-
ally the spruce became less dense, and on either side of
the trail, dark green ferns grew in abundance.

When Sarah caught sight of a distant carpet of delicate gentians, she paused to admire their deep blue
flowers. "It is a curious thing," she said, "how abundance can dull one's senses."

Her guide's brows lifted in question. "Your statement is certainly curious. Especially in this world of
more, more, more. So curious, in fact, that I must de-
mand an explanation. How has abundance dulled
your senses?"

"The flowers," she replied, pointing to the gentians.
"When I left town, the parks and gardens were in full
bloom, with blossoms of every kind and color vying
for one's attention, yet I passed them by with little
more than a glance. Now, here am I in this wild, majestic country, with marvelous views in every direction, and I find myself compelled to pause and admire
the brave little flower whose tenacity has helped it survive amid all this cool, rugged splendor."

"You are too hard on yourself, Miss Sterling. Perhaps your interest in the wildflowers is not a case of
dulled senses, but an example of your admiration for
bravery in the face of overwhelming odds."

This was such an accurate reading of her character
that Sarah was shocked into silence. How could he
know this of her? The question was neither asked nor
answered, because from somewhere overhead came
the loud, clear whistle of a curlew.

Immediately intrigued, Matthew cupped his hands
above his eyes to shield them from the sun while he
searched out the creature. "There he is," he said, pointing to their left.

Sarah slipped her arms through the braided vents

on either side of her cape so she could shield her eyes as Matthew had done, then looked where he indicated, watching the bird rise slowly on the air. "Your pardon, my feathered friend," she called to him, "did we frighten you?"

The bird whistled again, as if in answer to her question, and Matthew chuckled. "Curlews are normally rather shy birds, except when defending their young. Since they nest at this time of year, I suspect that resourceful fellow is attempting to entice us away from the hatchlings. Beguile us into following him."

"Friend curlew," she called again, "I, for one, should be happy to be enticed into that cloudless sky. I should dearly love to soar, unfettered, above the earth, free as the birds."

Feeling Matthew's gaze, Sarah turned to look at him, puzzled as to why he was watching her. "Should you not like to be beguiled, sir?"

A smile pulled at the corners of his mouth. "Madam, I already am."

At his softly spoken words, which Sarah knew instinctively had nothing to do with the bird, she experienced a strange, pleasantly unsteady feeling in her midsection. Though she told herself that he was only teasing her, she could not resist a peek into those enigmatic eyes. What she saw there made her breath catch in her throat, and for an insane moment, as their gazes met and held, she felt as if she were the only person who existed in his world.

Calling herself a fool for giving significance to an incident that was probably just another one of Matthew Donaldson's jests, she returned her attention to the curlew. "My friend," she called softly, "you may fly back to your young. You have nothing to fear from me."

"Fine words, Miss Sterling, from a woman who carries a pistol. Perhaps the news has gone abroad that you are armed and dangerous."

"Such fustian! As though I would ever shoot a wild animal."

"Oh?" he said, as if much struck by this information. "Would you not?"

"Of course not."

"No matter what the provocation from said wild animal?"

When she shook her head, he sighed dramatically. "Madam, you cannot know how that reassures me, for I have been living in some trepidation these two days and more, lest I provoke you into putting a bullet through my heart."

Somehow, she managed to restrain the smile that teased her lips. "Sir, I misspoke. What I meant to say was that I would never shoot a *forest* animal."

He laughed, and the warm, rich sound echoed deep in his chest. It was good laugh, and Sarah's heart beat a little faster knowing that he had found her amusing.

Of course, what female would not be flattered by attention from such a man. He was handsome enough to turn any woman's head, and intelligent into the bargain. And regardless of Lady Worthing's scathing remark about his having a taste for low company, Sarah could detect no sign of baseness in him.

From what she had observed, his character was worthy of esteem. Though a newly wealthy man, he had not rushed off to London to squander his inheritance in riotous living. Nor had he attempted to give himself airs—as well he might have done—to obscure a far from gentlemanly past. A past, moreover, that might have embittered a man with less integrity. He had been thrust into a harsh world when still little more than a boy, yet he had elected to learn from the experience when many another might have become vindictive and cursed the entire world for their misfortune.

Yes, there was much to admire in Matthew Donaldson.

"Come," he said, bringing her thoughts back to safer ground. "We cannot stand about here all afternoon, or we will never reach my special place."

His special place? Sarah would have sworn he said it was a *thing* he wished to show her. A masterpiece, actually.

To her surprise, he caught her hand in his and began walking rather hurriedly, obliging her to step lively as well. Not that she minded overmuch; she enjoyed the exercise, and his hand felt warm and strong as it held hers.

The entire time since passing the stables, they had been proceeding downhill, but now the descent seemed noticeably sharper, and somewhere not far away, Sarah heard the sound of swiftly flowing water.

"Careful," Matthew said, slowing his pace when a sandstone outcropping all but barred their way. "From here on, the ground is almost never dry and can be quite slippery."

Obliged to turn sideways to maneuver past the outcropping, he went first; then, holding her hand very tightly, he urged her to follow, adjuring her not to brush against the wet surface. Once she was past the barrier, he stepped aside and waited quietly for her reaction to what he had come to think of as *his* waterfall.

For a moment she said nothing, though her mouth opened in wonder as she lifted her head to see that spot twenty-five feet straight up where the falls began. The rushing water, as if impatient to reach its ultimate destination, dove over the edge of the mountain before tumbling down to the crystal clear stream below.

Fortunately, the wonder in her expressive brown eyes told him all he wanted to know, for when she finally spoke, her words were all but lost in the noise of the waterfall.

"Beautiful," he read upon her lips. Then he breathed a sigh of relief.

Since discovering this place several months ago, he had always visited it alone, not wanting to share it with anyone who might not appreciate it as he did. He loved not only the roaring splendor of the falls, but also the quiet stateliness of the boulders that stood in the streambed like vigilant sentinels, on guard against interlopers and Philistines. Of all he had inherited—the house, the lands, the art—it was this place he accepted most readily. This place spoke to his heart, told him he was home.

"So," he said, obliged to step close enough to speak directly into her ear, "it is as I thought. You are no Philistine."

She did not disappoint him by asking what he meant. Instead, she leaned toward him, her purpose to do as he had done and speak into his ear. Though she was obliged to place her hand on his chest to steady herself so she might stand on tiptoe. "How could anyone view such beauty and remain unmoved?" she asked. "You were correct, sir. This is a masterpiece."

Her warm breath sent a shock wave from Matthew's ear to his solar plexus, causing a reaction totally unwarranted by so innocent an act. As well, she stood so close he could almost feel her soft, feminine curves touching him. He had held her in his arms on two previous occasions, but those times he had caught her unaware. This time she had chosen to draw near to him, and though her actions were without guile, they set a pulse drumming inside his head.

Not wanting to spoil this moment of camaraderie, he ignored the voice within that bid him slip his arm around her and pull her against him, and with regret, he took a step back. It was as well, for at that exact moment, a trout fully two feet long leapt out of the center of the falls, claiming Sarah's attention.

With its yellow-brown tail fanning furiously back and forth, the fish sailed through the air, and when it landed in the stream below, Sarah hurried to the water's edge to assure herself that the creature was unharmed. It must have survived the plummet, for she looked back over her shoulder, a smile upon her soft lips.

They remained at the waterfall for no more than a quarter of an hour. Long before Sarah had seen her fill of the plunging water and the late-blooming Saxifrage that grew on the banks of the stream—the masses of bright yellow flowers resembling little rounded pyramids—Matthew motioned for her to come away, that it was time they returned to the Hall.

She took one last look at the falls before letting him assist her past the outcropping. Once on the other side, they reversed their route, following the trail to the spruce forest, and from there taking the footpath back to the stable area. Since the return trip was uphill the entire way, Sarah refrained from conversing, obliged to save her breath for the task of walking. Thankfully, Matthew had taken her hand again when they started back, for without his assistance she would have lagged behind.

Because Matthew did not talk, and Sarah could not, their arrival at the end of the path was unintentionally quiet, and when they stepped onto even ground, they almost collided with Mr. Noel Kemp. The handsome blond gentleman was pacing back and forth, as if waiting for someone.

"What the—" As surprised to see Matthew and Sarah as they were to encounter him, he swallowed his words just in time.

After taking a quick look over his shoulder, and seeing nothing, he seemed to regain his composure. "Well met," he said, favoring Sarah with a confident smile. "I recall that you declared yourself not particularly fond of horses, Miss Sterling. However, I did not expect your aversion to prompt you to walk all the way to the village."

"Sir?"

"That footpath," he said, the smile still in place. "The servants use it as a shortcut to Bellingham."

Obviously feeling that his presence there required an explanation, he said, "I, too, felt the need of a breath of fresh air. Unfortunately, I have not my cousin's luck. I did not find a lovely lady willing to accompany me."

"How strange," Matthew said, his tone sarcastic, "when I had it on good authority that at least one of the Worthing ladies was desirous of being shown about the estate."

To Sarah's surprise, Matthew's remark brought a flash of anger to the younger man's eyes.

"The ladies are resting up from the rigors of their journey," he said.

"Yes," Matthew agreed, "travel can be so very tiring. Especially when one is obliged to endure the ordeal of a well-sprung private chaise, with only four outriders to see to one's protection, and a host of obsequious innkeepers to see to one's comfort at every stop."

When Mr. Kemp's hands moved convulsively at his side, as if he contemplated making them into fists, Sarah spoke quickly, hoping to quell the animosity that seemed to be growing between the two gentlemen.

"We saw a waterfall!" she said. "And while we were there, a trout dove right out of the falls to land in the stream below." She spread her hands a full two feet apart. "You may well question my veracity, Mr. Kemp, but the fish was this big."

The gentleman relaxed his rigid posture. "I believe you, ma'am, for I used to fish there when I was a boy. A rather pretty spot, as I remember."

For some reason, Sarah did not wish to discuss that beautiful place with anyone who would label it "rather pretty." The word *Philistine* popped into her head, and she dared not look at Matthew Donaldson for fear he would know her thoughts. Instead, she waved her hand to encompass the dramatic scenery beyond the stables.

"I like this view as well," she said. "I had not been at Donmore Hall above two minutes when I decided that I should love to bring my colors out here to see if I could capture this marvelous vista on canvas."

"A capital idea, Miss Sterling, though I must warn you that you would not be the first to paint this particular scene. I must have seen at least a dozen renditions of this southern vista. Over the years, every lady who visited Donmore Hall sketched it, and each one seemed to think it necessary to have her efforts framed as a gift for my cousin Carlton."

Sarah could not recall seeing any such paintings. "Are they on display about the house, sir?"

"Oh, no, ma'am. They are up in the attic gathering dust and cobwebs. My cousin kept them all, fearful that one of the ladies might return one day and inquire after her gift."

Smiling, as though at a pleasant memory, he said, "When I was a boy, I used to sneak up to the attic on rainy days and rummage around. In addition to an old trunk filled with even older toys, and numerous pieces of discarded furniture, there were stacks of old frames and canvases to be looked through. Some of the paintings are quite atrocious, and I often laughed until my sides ached.

"Not," he continued quickly, "that I should expect any effort of yours to be less than charming."

This talk of paintings reminded Sarah that she had meant to ask Matthew Donaldson if there was a key to the gallery. "Sir," she said, "there is something I had meant to ask you earlier, only it slipped my mind."

"And it seems to have slipped my mind," Matthew said, "that you have walked several miles, and that your garments are probably wet from the spray of the falls. Pray, forgive me for making you stand about in the air, possibly taking a chill. May I suggest that we return to the house?"

He turned then to Noel Kemp. "As for you, Mr.— Cousin Noel—we will leave you to your solitary commune with nature."

Barely giving Sarah time to bid Mr. Kemp enjoy his stroll, Matthew put his hand beneath her elbow and led her up the flagstone path and straight to his book room. Since his hold on her arm was a bit firmer than was necessary, she took the hint that he wished her to remain silent until they were safely inside. When the French windows were shut behind them, he took the mantle from around her shoulders and motioned for her to sit in one of the red leather chairs close to the fire.

"Before you ask your question, may I send for some refreshments?"

"No, I thank you, sir. I wanted only to inquire if there is a key to the gallery."

"If there ever was one, I have not found it. I sent a message yesterday to the smithy in Bellingham, asking if he could make a new key. Unfortunately, he is visiting a neighboring village for a wedding, and until his return, the door must remain unlocked."

"I see," Sarah said, rising from the chair. "In that case, unless you have questions regarding the inventory, I will return to my work. I should like to get my supplies set up this afternoon, and decide which of the paintings is in most need of restoration, so I can begin work first thing tomorrow morning." She paused, giving him an opportunity to issue any instructions he might have.

"A moment," he said. Crossing over to the massive oak desk, he unlocked the drawer and withdrew the neatly penned sheets. After reading through a couple of descriptions, he said, "This grid thing, explain its significance to me."

She went to stand beside him, looking around his broad shoulders at the pages he held. "As you can see," she said, reaching around him to trace the lines with her finger, "these are the four walls of the gallery. I have attempted to represent each of the pictures on those walls—ovals, squares, and rectangles—giving a number to each for identification."

Using the grid and the topmost sheet of the inventory, she showed him the first number, then read aloud her description of the corresponding painting.

"Very logical," he said, glancing through each sheet, checking it against the grid. "What of these?" he asked, when he came to the final four numbers. "The shapes are numbered and represented on the grid, but you have written nothing about them in the inventory."

"That is because there is nothing to say. Those spaces are merely outlines on the wall where it appears pictures once hung."

"Four of them?" he asked.

"Yes, sir."

The muscle that had twitched in his jaw yesterday morning was back in action. "Show me," he said through clenched teeth.

Feeling his sudden tension, Sarah walked rapidly, preceding him through the library door and up the broad staircase, not slowing her pace until they were inside the gallery. "Over there," she said a bit breathlessly, pointing to the four small shapes that showed dimly against the muted cream of the walls.

"Damnation!"

This time Sarah did not bat an eye at his swearing; she was much too disturbed by the rigid set of his jaw. "What is it? Tell me, please. Did I do something wrong? If so, I can fix—"

"You did nothing," he said, the words clipped.

"Then what has made you so angry?"

"My own imprudence. I should have ordered that blasted key weeks ago."

"The key? What has the key to do with my grid?"

"With your grid, nothing. With my own carelessness, everything."

"I still do not understand."

"Actually, it is quite simple. It would appear that we do, indeed, have a thief in our midst, and he—or perhaps she—is more brazen than I had supposed."

He walked over and touched his hand to the wall, the fingers spread wide, as if to assure himself that nothing hung there. "Three days ago," he said, "when last I looked, there were only three blank spaces."

Chapter Seven

"You really must hire a French chef," Lady Worthing said, giving her attention to the gentleman who sat at the head of the mahogany dining table. "While female cooks are good enough for smaller homes, in an establishment such as Donmore Hall, the absence of a chef makes the family appear quite outré."

With a sigh of disdain, the lady placed her fork across her plate, abandoning the beefsteaks in oyster sauce after only one nibble, much as she had done when served the broiled fowl and mushrooms. As for the half-dozen removes, she refused to dignify those dishes with so much as a look. "If you are to entertain on a scale worthy of your position, Donaldson, you would do well to let yourself be guided by me in this matter. Hire a chef."

Matthew signaled the footman to remove her ladyship's plate. "Your pardon, Lady Worthing, but what can I have said that made you think I wished to entertain?"

"But surely you will not wish to become a hermit. I assure you, your wife would be desolate in such an isolated place as this without the comfort of an occasional party of friends."

Wife! Sarah almost choked on a bite of the mouthwatering beefsteak. As for the other members of the party, their reactions to the word, though not so dramatic as hers, were certainly telling.

Miss Chloe Worthing, who appeared even lovelier at close range than she had when Sarah had spied her from the gallery window, blushed to the roots of her dusky curls. As well, she lowered her long, thick lashes, a ploy that successfully hid whatever emotions might have been revealed by her big blue eyes.

As for Mr. Noel Kemp, a pulse beat visibly in that gentleman's temple, and as he stared at the lovely Chloe, who sat opposite him, he squeezed his wine-glass with such intensity that Sarah feared the fragile crystal might shatter in his hand, spilling the excellent bordeaux all over the fine linen tablecloth.

Matthew alone seemed undisturbed by talk of a wife. He merely smiled. "Lady Worthing—"

"Please," she said, a look of satisfaction upon her face, much like that of a cat who holds the family canary securely between its paws, "call me Cousin Agatha."

"Cousin Agatha," he continued, inclining his head as if in acknowledgment of a favor bestowed, "I must ask your pardon once more for any miscommunication between us. Though here again, I cannot think what I have said that would give you the impression that I wished to have a wife?"

At this remark, all four of his auditors gave him their undivided attention. Her ladyship, aghast at losing the imagined canary, sputtered. "But, but, sir. You must marry!"

"Must I? I cannot think why."

"Be . . . because you owe it to your name to set up your nursery as soon as possible. Otherwise, what would become of the estate, and the collection, should you meet with an accident."

He turned upon the lady a look that would have made a taproom bully rethink his dare. "Am I to meet with an accident?"

"No, no! At least I hope you do not." Her ladyship

toyed nervously with the garnets that circled her thin neck. "However, one never knows what may happen. The area is riddled with hares and their holes, and one hears of unwary horses stepping in those holes and tossing their riders."

"Ah, yes," he replied. "Hares. I thank you for the warning, ma'am, and if it will ease your mind, I promise to be on the watch for those pesky creatures. In the meantime, let me assure you that should anything happen to me, my will is in order."

This effectively stopped the conversation, for not even a grandam of Lady Worthing's audacity would have the effrontery to ask a gentleman what, or who, he had put in his will. After that, silence reigned.

The evening was going badly. But then, it had started out unfelicitously for Sarah.

Because she had stayed too long in the gallery, and was late going to her bedchamber to dress, the last gong had already sounded when she hurried into the drawing room where both the ladies and both the gentlemen were enjoying glasses of sherry.

"Ah, Miss Sterling," Matthew said, setting his glass upon the mantel and walking toward her.

"Sir," she said, "forgive my tardiness, I—"

"Became so lost in your work," he finished for her, "that you failed to hear the gong."

Upon perceiving the female employed to clean the paintings, Lady Worthing gasped, and in light of her poorly concealed displeasure, one might have been forgiven for thinking her ladyship had been asked to dine with the laundress.

From there, the evening worsened.

The gentlemen were unfailingly polite, and the lovely Chloe—beautifully attired in a gown of primrose Georgette trimmed at the sleeves with tiny satin rosebuds—had smiled sweetly at Sarah and vowed herself in awe of anyone brave enough to touch a painting by Rubens or Van Dyck. The kindness of the threesome notwithstanding, as the dinner progressed, Sarah wished she had obeyed her first impulse and had her meal brought to her room on a tray.

Now that her ladyship had tipped her hand by broaching the subject of marriage and the begetting of heirs, Sarah felt even more de trop, and she resolved to excuse herself the instant the sweets course was finished. That happy event occurred some quarter hour later, and when Lady Worthing rose from the table, giving the signal that the ladies should retire to the drawing room, Sarah made good her escape.

It was not to be wondered at that sleep eluded Sarah that night. While she lay upon her luxurious featherbed, tossing about with such frequency that her thick hair worked free of her night braid, her mind worked with the tenacity of a terrier, creating scenarios one after the other. The major theme of those imagined scenes concerned what was happening belowstairs, or more accurately, what might be happening between Chloe and Matthew.

In one scenario, Chloe played the pianoforte while Matthew turned the pages of the music for her, an admiring look upon his face. In another, Chloe asked clever, intuitive questions which Matthew answered willingly, that teasing light in his eyes. And always, Lady Worthing sat beside the fire, smiling at the handsome couple, content that her matchmaking was a success.

Not that Sarah blamed Matthew, or any man, for being taken with Chloe's beauty. After all, the young lady was stunning, well connected, and exactly the kind of female a wealthy gentleman would choose for his wife. Why this thought should cause Sarah to thrash about in her bed and resort to pounding her pillow in an attempt to find a position conducive of repose, she did not know. Nor, if the truth be known, did she wish to look too deeply into the matter.

Needing something to divert her thoughts from the images of Matthew Donaldson falling under the spell of Miss Chloe Worthing, Sarah tried to focus her attention upon the reason why she had come to Donmore Hall, which was to do a job of work, thereby earning money to help support herself and her ailing father. In time, thoughts of work led her to recall what Mr. Kemp had said that afternoon about the canvases in the attic.

Upon first hearing about those paintings, a rather fanciful idea had taken hold in Sarah's imagination—a notion that the thief might have stashed the missing paintings among the amateur works. The longer she thought about that possibility, the more determined she became to examine those canvases for herself. Since sleep continued to elude her, she decided there was no better time than the present.

While the case clock at the end of the corridor struck midnight, she threw back the covers and fetched her wrapper from the foot of the bed. Moving quietly so she did not disturb Morag, who slept in the dressing room adjoining the bedchamber, Sarah slipped her arms into the plain lawn wrapper, tied the ribbons at the neck and across the bosom, then lit the single candle that sat on her bedside table.

She did not waste time securing the hair that fell all about her face. After all, who would see her? Confident that she could go to the attic, examine the canvases, and return undetected, she held the candlestick aloft. Her mind resolute, she quit the room and tiptoed barefoot toward the backstairs that gave access to the top of the house.

Upon arriving at the uppermost floor of the house, Sarah found the narrow corridor uncarpeted and unlit, and for just a moment she contemplated returning to her bedchamber. Calling herself a coward for even thinking of being frightened away, she cupped her hand around the candle flame to protect it, and continued past the half-dozen doors to right and left. Aware that those doors gave access to the tiny rooms shared by the housemaids, she crept toward the slightly larger door directly ahead.

The only sound other than her own footfalls and the rhythmic hum of soft snores coming from one of the tiny rooms, was the loud thumping of her heart. The major aroma was that of camphor, a substance put up in little cloth bags to discourage insects and mice, and the closer she got to the attic proper, the stronger grew the sharp scent.

The two wooden steps that gave access to the storage area were nothing more than planks nailed into place, and they were rough beneath her feet. Still, she continued, undaunted, and as her hand touched the latch, she congratulated herself on conquering her fear and on her success at stealth. After exercising extreme caution in opening the door, lest it creak, she almost spoiled everything by screaming at sight of a dressmaker's dummy that stood just inside the room.

"Heaven help me," she said, once her breathing slowed to its normal pace, "what is that?"

Sarah took a good look at the form. It wore a rusty, puce satin dress over wide, old-fashioned panniers, and someone had stuffed a gentleman's moth-eaten peruke with rags then fastened the wig atop the form to simulate a head.

"Are you merely a young boy's trick," she asked, "or are you the work of an adult mind, one hoping to frighten away unwanted investigation?" She hoped it was the former. However, no matter who had set the antiquated lady on guard, they had not accomplished their goal, for now Sarah was more determined than ever to see what secrets the attic might hold.

After placing the candlestick on a wobbly table, she made a cursory search of the contents of two water-stained old sea chests before moving on to the canvases stacked against the wall. There were at least three-dozen artistic attempts abandoned there. Some were set in handsome gilded frames—those gifts to Mr. Carlton Donaldson, no doubt—while others retained their original, unadorned states.

One at a time, Sarah took those rejected efforts to the light so she might examine them. Though one or two showed promise of talent on the artist's part, most were rather poor attempts, and she could well believe that a young boy might find them a cause for laughter. There were, indeed, numerous depictions of the southern view, and of those, one in particular made her chuckle. It was an excruciatingly stilted watercolor dated forty-five years ago and signed by none other than Agatha Donaldson.

"Ah," Sarah said, still smiling, "I wonder if Lady Worthing would be interested in seeing this after all these years?"

Sarah decided against exposing the lady to ridicule, and as she set the canvas among those already examined, her attention was caught by one of the final two paintings. The first was another stable view, and she did not even bother taking it to the light, but the other was a copy of one of the works in the gallery: the young boatman with the tasseled blue cap.

Though it was rather well done, the copy would not have fooled a dealer or a knowledgeable buyer, not for a minute. Even in this dim light, Sarah could see that the rich texture of the original was missing. Also, the old masters mixed their own paints and kept the formulas to themselves, jealously guarding their secret mixtures. For that reason, their colors were difficult to copy. In this particular instance, the blue of the boat-

man's hat contained a bit too much green, and the boat
in which he stood needed just a touch more bronze.

Sarah put the canvas back against the wall, convinced that the copy was nothing more than some
young lady's way of passing the long days spent at
Donmore Hall. If anyone had hoped to switch a coun-
terfeit for the original, surely they would have chosen
a more believable facsimile.

Disappointed to find nothing revealing—no hidden
copies waiting to be exchanged for the originals, no
stolen paintings rolled up and hidden in out-of-the-
way corners—she returned to the table and retrieved
the candlestick. Her notion that the thief might have
stashed the missing paintings among the amateur
works had been a foolish fancy, and now that she
knew just how foolish, she was grateful she had not
voiced her suspicion to anyone. She was equally grateful that no one would ever know she had been up
here.

It was while she stepped around the panniered
dressmaker's dummy that Sarah saw something she
had not noticed earlier, probably because of her fright
at encountering the supposed lady. Something lay in a
small heap not far from the door, and when Sarah held
the candle aloft, the heap was revealed to be four small
picture frames. All four were empty. Three of the
frames were liberally covered in cobwebs, as though
they had been lying in the attic for weeks or possibly
months, but the fourth frame, though dusty, showed
no sign of the gossamer webs.

The master bedchamber was across the corridor
from the gallery, and until a new key could be made
for the gallery door to lock out whoever was helping
himself to the paintings, Matthew Donaldson had resolved to sleep with the door to his room ajar. Not that
he had gotten any sleep since bidding good night to

his three uninvited guests, for he had chosen to remove only his coat, his waistcoat, and his boots before stretching out on the large, full tester bed.

As the night grew long, he had begun to drift into a half-sleeping, half-waking state, only to be roused from his slumber when the case clock struck midnight. Scarce two minutes later, he thought he heard the soft click of a door being shut in the east wing. Moving quickly, he reached for the pistol he had left primed and ready on the bedside table, and without bothering with a candle or his boots, he walked quietly toward the stealthy sound.

A squeak on the back stairs told him he had not imagined that someone was abroad, but he kept a discreet distance, not wanting to tip his hand before he discovered who was sneaking about at this hour. Spying a glimmer of light reflected on the wall at the top of the stairwell, he followed it. This time he was a bit too discreet and let the person get too far ahead of him. He reached the topmost floor just in time to see the attic door shut, plunging the narrow corridor into almost complete darkness.

As ill luck would have it, while he inched soundlessly across the bare floor, the door to one of the servants' rooms opened, and he was obliged to duck into the dark corner to the left of the rough wooden stairs. He cursed himself for a fool, for if there was one thing he did not need, it was to be caught sneaking about at night near the maids' rooms! He might not be a gentleman in the strictest sense of the word, but neither was he a lecher, and he had no wish to figure as one of those despicable men who pursued the female servants.

A young housemaid appeared in the doorway, and while she looked to the left and right to make certain the corridor was empty, someone inside the room giggled. "Shh," she cautioned. "You want me to get

caught? That old stiff rump, Bailey, would like nothing better than to give me the sack."

The only answer was another giggle.

The girl wore a shawl over her night rail, and her
hair was in curl papers, and in her left hand she carried a chipped saucer containing the stub of a work
candle. Thankfully, the light was too dim to reveal
Matthew's hiding place, but he remained still as a post
just in case.

"What if there's a bit of trifle left from supper?" the
maid asked of whoever was inside the room. "You
want I should bring you sommit?"

"Ooh!" squealed the unseen female, "now that'ud
be something like! If it b'aint gobbled up already by
one or other of them gluttonous footmen, then fill the
bowl to the rim and bring two spoons."

Both girls giggled, then the one with the candle stub
hurried off toward the stairs. Unfortunately, she did
not close the door to the room she shared, so Matthew
was obliged to remain in his dark corner or risk discovery.

The maid had been gone about five minutes when
Matthew heard muffled noises coming from inside the
attic—sounds not unlike that of small furniture being
moved. A minute later, he heard the door latch being
lifted from the other side.

After being in the dark for so long, he blinked at the
candlelight, but it needed only a moment for his eyes
to grow accustomed to the sudden illumination. Not
that he needed more than a glance to recognize the
person who stepped cautiously down the two rough
wooden steps. It was Sarah Sterling, and though
Matthew was not at all surprised to find her there, he
was more than a bit disconcerted by her appearance.

Her feet were bare, and her russet hair had come
loose from its braid and now rippled about her shoulders, reminding him of the waterfall when the reflec-

tion of the westering sun turned it to fire. But the thing he found most disturbing was her attire, for only a night rail and a thin wrapper stood between her and nakedness.

"Is that you, Betsy?" the girl in the room called in a loud whisper.

At the sound of the girl's voice, Sarah paused at the bottom of the steps, her heart in her throat. Having come to the attic on a fool's errand, she definitely did not wish to be caught by one of the servants. How would she possibly explain her presence? When no likely explanation occurred to her, she decided that her wisest course of action would be to hide in the corner until the maid went back to sleep.

Since discovery was preferable to lurking in a corner with a possible nest of mice, she turned and held the candle aloft to make certain her chosen spot was free of inhabitants. What she saw there made her long for a couple of innocuous rodents.

Matthew Donaldson stood mere inches from her, and for a fraction of a second she stared speechlessly at him. He glowered back at her, not nearly as surprised to see her as she was to see him, and from the look on his face, he would have liked nothing better than to use the pistol he held in his hand. Before she could think of anything remotely intelligent to say to convince him not to shoot her, he blew out the flame of her candle and snaked his arm around her waist, pulling her into the darkness with him.

When her back touched the cold wall, she gasped. "What are you—"

"Not now," he muttered. "They will hear you."

"Betsy?" called the girl again.

"Coming," came the distant reply. Seconds later a dim glow showed at the top of the back stairs. As the maid came nearer, Matthew Donaldson stepped between Sarah and the approaching light, using his broad back to shield her from possible view. The hand holding the pistol he kept by his side, the weapon pointed downward, but his left hand he placed on the wall, just above Sarah's shoulder.

"Was there trifle?" the girl asked. "Did you bring some?"

"I got it," Betsy whispered. Before the young maid entered the small bedroom, she looked behind her nervously. "But I'd swear there was eyes watching me all the while."

"You're that daft, Betsy Mullins. Next you'll be telling me you saw ghosts hiding in the corners."

Whatever Betsy's reply, it was lost forever, for the door clicked shut, and with its closing, near darkness engulfed the tiny corridor once again.

Sarah breathed a sigh of relief, happy they had not been discovered. "It was only one of the maids," she whispered, "pilfering a late-night snack."

"Caution," he replied softly. "Give them time to settle in."

In the dimness she could see little more than the outline of Matthew's head and shoulders, but she knew when he turned to look behind him, for when he moved, his bare foot brushed the side of hers. Sarah's breath caught in her throat. Her feet were cold, but his skin was unbelievably warm. Neither of them moved, and the unexpected contact of flesh upon flesh seemed unimaginably intimate, making little prickly sensations run up her spine.

Pure foolishness, she told herself. All she need do to break the contact was to ease her foot back an inch. She remained perfectly still. "They are gone," she said. "Perhaps we should go."

His hand was still near her shoulder, but when she spoke, he bent his elbow and rested his forearm on the wall instead, bringing them that much closer. "Or," he murmured, "we could stay here. They might come out again."

The lazy quality of his voice mesmerized her, making her feel lazy as well, and when he did not move away, but caught a lock of her hair and brushed it across his lips, she knew he was not at all concerned about being discovered.

"Mmm," he said softly. "Your hair smells good. Like lilacs after the rain."

"It does?" she asked, entranced as much by the unexpected compliment as by his nearness.

When he would have leaned even closer, she put her hand up to slow his progress, but to her surprise, she encountered not the coat she expected but the soft lawn of his shirt. The neck of the garment was open, and her fingertips touched the hard column of his throat. The initial contact was accidental; the second was not. Of its own free will, her palm flattened against his chest, and she felt the beat of his heart.

It was exhilarating to be privy to the rhythm of another person's life force, and when she relaxed her restraining wrist, allowing him to move close enough to nuzzle her forehead with his chin, she felt the tempo of his heart accelerate, causing a similar increase in the pounding inside her own chest. Energy emanated from his body, and his nearness made her all too aware that she wore nothing but her nightclothes.

When he spoke, his voice was slightly husky. "Your skin smells even better than your hair. I find the fragrance more intoxicating than wine."

She was thinking the same thing about him. The tangy aroma of his shaving soap acted upon her like a drug, and she experienced the oddest desire to press her face against his strong neck.

As well, his nearness was having a strange effect upon her knees; they felt as if they might give way beneath her at any moment, making her long to slip her arms around his waist to keep from falling. It was a hypnotic idea, but before Sarah could act upon it, some last shred of sanity made itself heard, reminding her of Matthew Donaldson's earlier warning.

He had told her how he might act if they were constantly thrown in one another's path. Unfortunately, he had said nothing of how *she* might react. That reaction, she realized, was the real danger. Convinced she had better walk away while her limbs would still support her weight, she pushed gently against his chest.

"No one is coming," she whispered. "I think we can leave now."

He grew very still.

"I must go," she said.

"Of course," he replied after a moment, then he pushed away from the wall.

When they walked down the dark corridor toward the stairs, he held her arm, not letting it go until they reached the floor below. Sarah thought he would ask for some sort of explanation as to why she was in the attic, but he did not. All he said was, "I will watch you safely to your room. We will talk tomorrow."

"Yes, sir."

She turned to walk away, but he stopped her. "Miss Sterling?"

"Yes, sir."

"Miss Worthing wishes to see Hadrian's Wall. Or rather, her aunt declared the girl wishful of seeing it. Therefore, an outing is planned for tomorrow. I would like you to accompany us."

"Thank you, sir, but I have work to do, and—"

"Madam," he said, his voice brusque, "it was not a request."

Sarah could not imagine why he wished her to be one of the party. Nevertheless, he was still her employer, and considering all the things she had done to give him cause to dismiss her, it behooved her to try for a bit of meekness.

"I shall be happy to go," she said.

"And, Miss Sterling?"

"Yes, sir."

"Promise me you will not do any more midnight exploring."

"But, sir, I—"

"Promise me," he said. "Surely you see now what trouble it can lead to."

Chapter Eight

Lady Worthing was not an early riser. Having done her duty the previous evening by extracting a promise from Matthew that he would take Chloe to see Hadrian's Wall, she obviously saw no reason to bestir herself before noon that day. For that reason, Sarah entered the bright green-and-white breakfast room at a quarter past eight to find Miss Chloe Worthing in the sole company of Mr. Noel Kemp.

The lady and gentleman were deep in conversation, else they would have noticed Sarah's arrival in time to don masks of indifference. Since they were initially unaware of her presence, they continued in what appeared suspiciously like a quarrel.

"You have only to show a bit of fortitude," Mr. Kemp said. "She cannot force you to do anything you find abhorrent." He paused, but when she said nothing, he continued. "That is, if you *do* find it abhorrent."

The young lady sniffed. "Noel, how can you be so horrid? You know how I feel about— Oh!" she said, discovering Sarah standing just inside the room.

"Your pardon," Sarah said. "The door was ajar, else you would have heard me enter."

While the young lady pressed a lace handkerchief to her damp eyes, Mr. Kemp pushed back his chair and stood, bestowing upon Sarah a smile sunny enough to distract most any female's attention. "Good morning, Miss Sterling. The dishes of the buffet are excellent, and I can personally recommend the poached cod and the coffee, both of which are first rate. Or perhaps you would prefer tea and a currant bun if yours is a more delicate palate."

Sarah chuckled as if his pun had been intentional. "Neither my palate nor my palette are particularly fragile, sir, but I thank you for your concern."

The gentleman stared, uncomprehending for just a moment, then he laughed aloud. "Oh! I say, Miss Sterling, you are quick."

"Perhaps too quick," Matthew Donaldson said from the doorway.

Like Sarah, he had entered the room unnoticed, but now all eyes turned his way, Sarah's most reluctantly. She had been afraid that she would be embarrassed when next she saw him. If the truth be known, she had lain awake in her bed until dawn showed its pale pink face at the edge of the window hangings, wondering how she should act.

In the minutes just before she fell asleep, she came to terms with the fact that what had happened between her and her employer had meant nothing to him. Not only had he told her from the beginning that he was likely to amuse himself with whatever female was close at hand, but he was also a man who indulged in the occasional jest. In flirting with her, he was only continuing his little joke, so she resolved to act toward him as if nothing had happened.

Of course, when she made that resolution she had not counted on his looking so devastatingly handsome that she could do nothing but stare at him like the village dolt gawking at a raree show. Not that she faulted him, or any man, for making himself as attractive as possible, but there was a limit!

A man of his height and build should not wear a coat that fit his broad shoulders to such perfection, nor should he be allowed to don pantaloons that revealed the firm yet supple muscles of his thighs and calves. As for the Spanish blue superfine of his coat, that was the outside of enough! The color should be forbidden him altogether; especially when it was seen that the blue gave the gentleman's gray eyes the mysterious silver hue of a winter sea.

"Too quick?" Mr. Kemp repeated, a slight edge to his voice. "Cousin, are you one of those men who dislikes wit in a female?"

"Not at all," replied their host, choosing to ignore the younger man's tone. "I appreciate intelligence wherever I find it. For instance," he said, acknowledging the lovely Chloe with a brief bow, "I see Miss Worthing was wise enough to choose a substantial breakfast, for ours will be a long day.

"However," he added, looking meaningfully at the plate of coddled eggs and shaved ham that sat untouched before her, "she has not so far proved her wisdom by partaking of the food."

While the young lady picked up her fork, Matthew gave his attention to the dozen covered dishes on the sideboard. Taking one of the gold-rimmed China plates stacked there, he served up small portions of sheared eggs, cod, and aspic, then handed the filled plate to Sarah.

"Eat up, Miss Sterling," he said, preceding her to the oval rosewood table and pulling out a chair for her. "Though your day will not be quite so exacting as Miss Worthing's, you will have need of your strength. Angus Newsome, who has been steward at the Hall for more than twenty years, informs me that the walk along the section of Hadrian's Wall to which we go stretches fully fifteen miles."

Sarah paused in the act of placing her napkin in her lap, surprise writ plainly upon her face. "Fifteen miles! Sir, if you should load my plate with a sampling of every dish on the sideboard, I could not walk half that number of miles.''

"What is this?'' Mr. Kemp asked, even more surprised than Sarah. "Is Miss Sterling to go with you and Chloe? Will you be a party of three?''

Matthew looked at the other man, his face a study in innocence. "A party of three? What can you mean, sir? Do not tell me you have decided not to go along. Really, Kemp, this is too, too vexing. There is Miss Worthing looking as refreshing as a summer's day in her riding habit. And—by the way, ma'am, what is that color? Pistache?''

Not giving her time to answer, he continued. "And here is Miss Sterling who, as you know, does not ride. I cannot be in two places at once, my good man. Either I drive Miss Sterling, leaving Miss Worthing unattended, or I ride with Miss Worthing, leaving Miss Sterling to tool the curricle and pair as best she can.''

Two days ago, Sarah would have protested loudly at the suggestion that she drive a sporting vehicle about the countryside, but she was beginning to know Matthew Donaldson a little, so she merely gave him a speaking glance before applying herself to her meal. Whatever his purpose, she knew they were all three merely pawns in his scheme, so she chose to eat while he completed his machinations.

Mr. Kemp had returned to his place at the table, and now he stalled for time by taking a sip of coffee. "How about this,'' he said, setting the translucent cup in its saucer. "Since I am not familiar with your team, cousin, how would it be if *I* rode with Chloe . . . I mean Miss Worthing . . . while you drove Miss Sterling?''

Matthew brought his plate to the table and pulled out a chair. "It sounds like a workable plan, Kemp. What say you, Miss Sterling? Have you any objections to the scheme?''

It was three-quarters of an hour later before she answered his question, and by that time she was seated beside Matthew in the curricle, and he had just given the very fresh team of matched blood bays the office to be upon their way.

"I protest," he said, "for I asked if you had any objections. At the time you said nothing."

"Naturally I did not, for to do so would have made Mr. Kemp look no-how for having fallen into your trap. I am not so unkind, sir."

"Madam," he said, "you are truly a—"

"Pawn?" she asked.

"Martyr," he finished, not in the least discomposed by her tirade.

Sarah remained silent for a moment, watching Matthew handle the ribbons with ease. He kept the bays on the meandering carriageway, then guided them past the gatehouse and through the wrought-iron gateposts as though they were not the high-strung, eager creatures they were. "I suppose I should be grateful I was not obliged to tool that pair."

He gave his attention to the horses as they turned right and began to trot alongside the black stone wall, his only reaction to Sarah's remark a slight movement at the corner of his mouth.

"To return to your very solicitous inquiry as to whether or not I had any objections to the final scheme," she continued, "you know full well that it is Lady Worthing who will have the objections. Cold, scathing objections, I should think. And if she makes you a gift of every last one of them, repeating herself often, you will have come by your just deserts."

"Speaking of desserts," he said, "if you will forgive *my* pun, puts me in mind of those two giggling maids and their filched trifle."

Sarah could not believe he had brought up the subject that had prompted last night's debacle. She felt the heat rush to her face. So much for her resolve to treat the entire incident as though nothing had happened.

"Something occurred to me later, Miss Sterling, and I thought I had better ask you about it."

Here it was! He wanted to know what she was doing rummaging around in his attic. Not that he did not have every right to be informed about what went on in his own house. "Yes, sir," she said. "What did you wish to know?"

"Did you get splinters in your toes?"

"Sir?"

"From those two steps leading to the attic? Though one can hardly call them steps. They are little more than unfinished planks, actually. The thing is, if I had known the attic was such a popular place, and that young ladies would be tiptoeing up and down those rough steps without their shoes, I would have had them replaced earlier."

Not certain she had heard him correctly, she studied the strong profile. Again, Sarah thought she saw his lips twitch, and she began to wonder if he was toying with her.

"Have them replaced?" she said. "To what do you refer? The steps? Or the young ladies?"

This time he could not school his face, and a smile parted his well-shaped lips. "The steps, madam. Definitely the steps. How should I do without the young ladies? Without them, I should be obliged, on misty days, to remain by the fire in my book room instead of stumbling about out-of-doors.

"And let us not forget last evening when, after I had partaken of a tedious dinner with people I did not invite to join me, then endured an even more tedious hour waiting for the tea tray to arrive so I could escape to my bedchamber, I was *not* obliged to remain in my bed the entire night. Were it not for a certain young lady getting up to her old tricks, I should have missed entirely the opportunity to roam about the darkened house, a pistol in my hand, in search of possible thieves."

A tedious hour spent waiting for the tea tray?

Every word he had spoken after that interesting remark fell upon deaf ears. The hour had been tedious. Even with the beautiful Chloe Worthing to look at, he had found the evening tedious.

What an interesting word, tedious. Oddly, just letting the syllables echo in her mind lifted Sarah's spirits and gave her the confidence to confess to her snooping.

"I thank you, sir, for your concern on behalf of my toes. Fortunately, I was not subjected to even one splinter. However, as a result of my brief—and, I confess, unauthorized—sojourn in your attic, my hair was liberally dusted with cobwebs. When I beheld my image in the looking glass, I resembled nothing so much as some old crone wearing a powdered wig."

"On that assessment, madam, we must agree to differ."

"I . . . I was not fishing for compliments, sir."

"Nor did I give one. I merely stated a truth the looking glass would have told you had you looked more closely."

Sarah felt a renewal of that breathlessness she had experienced last night when they were alone in the dark; when he had lifted her hair to his lips; when she had longed to put her arms around him. Thankfully, this time she was in no danger of succumbing to such temptation. This time they were in broad daylight, and the gentleman was not so close she could smell that masculine scent that clung to his skin, or feel his heart beating beneath her palm.

Logic told her that as long as she stayed away from dark corners, and made certain she was not so foolish as to reach out and touch him, she was safe. Perfectly safe. He could tease her all he wanted now, and she would remain impervious to his person and his charm.

"May one ask," he said, "if you found anything other than cobwebs in the attic?"

"I found only what Mr. Kemp had foretold—a stack of rather amateurish paintings. Oh," she said, recalling her discovery near the door, "I found the frames that had once held the four stolen paintings."

After a brief discussion of the empty frames, they agreed to say nothing more of the art collection—either the missing paintings or those still hanging on the walls—for Mr. Kemp and Miss Worthing had reined in their mounts just up the lane and were waiting for the curricle.

Their horses perfectly suited the handsome couple. Mr. Kemp, a blond Adonis, was astride a magnificent black gelding he called Sultan, while Miss Worthing sat as dainty as a fairy princess upon the back of a roan mare named Tempest. "Though, I assure you," the girl had confided before they left Donmore Hall, "it is a misnomer. Tempest is a sweet little goer with the gentlest disposition imaginable. A filly even you might like, Miss Sterling."

Sarah had mumbled some platitude, then hurried over to the curricle before Chloe offered to exchange places with her.

Now, as Matthew Donaldson drew up beside the waiting couple, Sarah noted that all evidence of their previous quarrel was gone. The young lady's eyes, tear-filled only that morning, shone with the glowing good health of youth and some other quality Sarah took leave to label as love. Not that she voiced her suspicion, of course. Still, a person would have to be dull-witted, indeed, not to notice the adoring looks Chloe lavished upon her companion when she thought no one else was attending.

As for the object of the young lady's affection, Mr. Noel Kemp did not care who deduced what from his glances. He was in love with the beauty, and he made no effort to conceal the fact.

Of course, Sarah was not such a romantic that she believed their mutual *tendres* were all that was needed to add 'happily ever after' to their biographies. Chloe Worthing was a marriageable female of uncommon beauty, and such loveliness was traditionally bestowed upon a man in possession of riches, power, or both. Noel Kemp possessed neither of those essentials. His good looks and charm notwithstanding, he was a gentleman who had been deprived of the estate and fortune he had been reared to think of as his, and without wealth or property, his chances of securing the hand of the beauty were nonexistent.

"I am trusting you, Kemp," Matthew said, "to know the best place for the securing of our cattle. You were, I presume, a frequent visitor to the wall during your boyhood sojourns in Bellingham."

"I should rather think I was!"

The ride through the countryside with his beloved had smoothed the rough edges from the gentleman's temper, and Noel answered with a degree of indulgence not previously shown his relative. "Only think of it. A lad, a Roman wall, the ghosts of veritable legions of Roman soldiers, and the centuries-old shouts of the Scots as they attacked the garrisons. 'Tis the stuff young boys' dreams are made of."

"Unquestionably," Matthew agreed.

Sarah and Chloe exchanged knowing looks, while Mr. Kemp continued. "I visited Northumberland frequently enough to know that each summer, when the holiday visitors begin to arrive for a view of the wall, groups of local citizens set up booths in a grassy meadow near the remains of one of the Roman garrison forts. For a fee, they will supply everything a person needs: guides, refreshments, accommodations for the cattle, and a place suitable for ladies to rest."

"Sounds just what we need. And they are set up this summer, do you think?"

He nodded, then pointed up the road. "We should come upon them within a half mile or so."

Not more than five minutes later, when they rounded a bend in the road, Sarah saw the booths in the distant meadow. There were a dozen of them clustered together, and in some ways they resembled a country fair, with brightly painted signs depicting the wares for sale: meat or fruit pies, lemonade or cider, and home brew.

There was one rather large tent, across the front of which was affixed an awning about four feet deep and eight feet wide. Half a dozen ladder-back chairs were arranged beneath the awning, offering shade during the summer months, and above the folded flap that served as a door was a sign printed in bold, black letters. The sign read, LADIES, ADMITTANCE ONEPENCE. Across the way, a similar, though much smaller tent, bore the word GENTLEMEN.

In a grassy area near a shallow stream, an enterprising farmer had roped off a quarter of an acre that now held two farm wagons, parked side by side, and four large workhorses, Percherons mostly, which were secured to pegs hammered into the ground, The Donmore party had not yet reached the roped-off area when a gangly lad of about twelve came running to catch hold of Sultan's bridle. "See to yer horse, mister?" he called. "Sixpence for the whole day."

A slightly younger lad, the first boy's brother—if the same disheveled, hay-colored hair and the same scattering of freckles were anything to judge by—latched on to the little mare's rein and began leading her toward the Percherons. "This way, ma'am."

"Can I lead yer team?" asked a soft, shy voice. "I know how."

From the high seat of the curricle, Sarah looked down upon a little girl with the same hair and freckles as the boys, but with the biggest, bluest eyes she had ever seen. The girl could not have been above six, little more than a baby herself, and rail thin, yet she balanced a little boy of about two on her hip.

"Get away from there, Dorrie!" the older boy shouted. "The gen'lman don't want ye scaring his cattle."

"But I can do it," insisted the little girl. She raised pleading eyes toward Sarah. "I'll do it for tuppence, ma'am."

"Give over, Dorrie!" barked the younger lad. "Pa says ye're just to tend Alfie, on account of that's all ye're good at. Girls don't know how to do nothing worth getting paid for."

The older boy grabbed the little girl by her arm and pulled her out of the way, then he touched his forelock respectfully to Matthew. "Don't mind her, yer honor. Just follow me if you will, and I'll see to the team quick as I get this here black took care of."

The little girl swung the child around to her other hip then hurried away, and while Sarah watched the departing figures, she experienced an unexpected fellow feeling for the waif with the big eyes. She knew what it was like to be told, simply because of her gender, that she was not talented enough to earn her own way, and she wished she had thought to bring her reticule with her. She had little enough money to share, but she could have spared twopence.

Matthew Donaldson was unusually quiet while he pulled the team into the designated area then helped Sarah from the curricle, and only after he watched Mr. Kemp and Miss Worthing hurry toward an excavation of one of the old garrison walls—Milecastles, the younger man called them—did he speak. "Since our companions have chosen to investigate on their own, Miss Sterling, you and I may please ourselves as to our route."

He tossed a half-guinea to one of the waiting guides to cover the cost of the tour, then he returned his attention to Sarah. "You need walk only as far as you like, ma'am, and should you grow tired, or feel a chill, you must promise to tell me."

"I shall keep that in mind," she said, adjusting the shallow brim of her straw bonnet against the sun's bright rays. Because the day was unusually balmy, she had chosen to wear her peach muslin frock, buttoning over it the forester green faille spencer she had got from the dressmaker a fortnight ago. Thanks in part to the new spencer, she felt positively stylish as she took the arm Matthew offered her and walked toward the north-facing rampart upon which was built the great gray stone barrier known as Hadrian's Wall.

"The long stone battlement," the guide began in a singsong manner, "sealed off the northwest frontier of the Roman Empire. Built between one hundred twenty-two and one hundred thirty AD, by order of Emperor Hadrian, the wall crosses the whole of northern England from coast to coast, stretching seventy-three miles from the Tyne Estuary on the east to Solway Firth on the west."

While the man proceeded with the speech he would probably repeat hundreds of times before summer's end, Sarah held Matthew's hand, allowing him to assist her up the steep basalt scarp. When they reached the parapet, she stared in wonder at the vastness of the landscape beyond. As if sensing that they wished for quiet, the guide broke off his running commentary and walked some piece away from them, squatting down on his heels to wait until they called him again.

Once the man had ceased his chatter, a quiet de-

scended upon the entire area, and Sarah breathed a
sigh of contentment as she slowly scanned the
panorama that stretched for untold miles. There was a
sense of remoteness about the place that was peaceful
rather than lonely, and in the distance, glacial lakes
dotted the landscape, sparkling in the sunshine like
tiny diamonds spilled on an unfurled bolt of green velvet.

From out of nowhere, a merlin appeared in the sky,
its slate blue underside clearly visible as the small
hawk paused, seemingly suspended in the air, supported by its outspread tail. A fitting addition to the
silent majesty of its surroundings, the bird made not a
sound. After a time, it quivered its wings almost imperceptibly, then without apparent effort, it suddenly
bore right and sailed from view, leaving Sarah sighing
at the precision of its flight.

"From this moment," Sarah whispered, "any sight
would be second best."

Matthew did not disappoint her by asking her
meaning. Instead, he said, "Then let us leave now,
madam, before lingering sullies the perfection of the
memory."

If their guide was disappointed that they remained
upon the wall for scarce half an hour, he was pleased
upon their return to the rest area to have another half-
guinea tossed his way.

Because they were obliged to wait for the return of
Mr. Kemp and Miss Worthing, Sarah and Matthew
strolled through the cluster of booths, glancing at the
many jams, preserves, and crafts presented for sale.
Pausing by a booth displaying little animals cunningly
carved from wood, Matthew asked if he might procure
some refreshments for her. "Cider? Lemonade?" Then,
with a wink, "Or a pie, perhaps?"

"A pie?" Sarah shuddered.

She knew he was teasing her, but the very thought of eating one of those greasy turnovers whose scent filled the air made her decidedly queasy. Her aversion to the pastries dated from an incident in her childhood, when her father took her to the annual May fair in town. Like many an eight-year-old, she wanted to taste everything offered for sale. The final treat—following close on the heels of two ices, a paper twist of marzipan, a hot-cross bun, and a ginger tea cake—was a meat pie. The effect of all that food on a young stomach was as disheartening as it was predictable, and as a result, Sarah had formed a sincere aversion to the pieman's wares.

"Thank you," she said, "but I do not care for anything. Actually—"

She stopped talking, for Matthew was not listening; his attention was focused on the little girl they had seen earlier. She was just a few feet away, beside one of the pie booths. Her eyes were closed, and she rested her back against the side of the booth, as if she were tired. The little boy was still perched on her hip, but his chin had fallen forward on his chest as though he napped.

For a time Matthew seemed to be considering something; then, without a word of warning, he put his hand beneath Sarah's elbow and steered her straight toward the two children. "I cannot help it," he said rather loudly, his tone almost angry, "this is not London, and I am not a magician. I cannot make tasters appear out of thin air."

Sarah wondered if he had gone daft from too much sun, for he stopped at the booth and began to look all around, as though hunting for something. "Oh, little girl," he said, his tone implying that he had only just noticed her standing there, "I wonder if you can help me?"

The child had straightened away from the booth

when she heard Matthew's approach, his voice angry, and now she stared at him, her blue eyes almost too big for her thin face. Wary beyond her years, she was obviously ready to flee if he should turn violent. "Me, sir?"

"Yes. I was just wondering where the tasters are."

The little girl blinked. "The what, sir?"

"You know," he said, "the people who taste food for ladies and gentlemen. This lady," he said, indicating Sarah, "was wishful of trying one of those delicious smelling pies, but hers is a delicate palate, and since she forgot to bring her taster along with her, there is no one to tell her if the beef is too salty."

The little girl resembled a rabbit surprised by a fox in the field, and as she tried to decide whether to run away or to remain and try to bluff it out, Matthew said, "Here is an idea. Perhaps *you* would consent to be the lady's taster."

Without waiting for the child's reply, he turned once again to Sarah. "How much do you usually pay your taster, my dear?"

Though every bit as perplexed by this conversation as the child, Sarah had one advantage, she knew Matthew Donaldson. "Pay?" she said, stalling for time. "I, er, never give less than, er—"

"Tuppence?" he suggested.

"Tuppence?" she repeated.

Suddenly recalling the earlier scene with the horses, Sarah discerned her part in this play. "Yes, yes, tuppence. Of course, if the *female* is really good at her job, I have been known to give her twice that amount."

The little girl gasped. "The tasters be females?"

"Oh, yes," Matthew replied. "It takes a woman, or in some instances a girl, to be a really successful taster. Males are no good at it. You understand how it is, you females being so much better at some things than we menfolk are."

Much struck by this new view of her sex, she chewed her lip as if doing so aided her mental processes. "And you say those Lunnon tasters, they get money for it?"

"Of course," Matthew said. "If the workman—or woman—is worthy of his hire. What say you? Will you try the pies and tell the lady which is best?"

"What if yer missus don't like the one I choose?"

Missus! Sarah might have known she would wind up being embarrassed. However, if her employer felt any similar discomfort at having been assigned a wife, he gave no sign of it.

"She will like it," he assured the child, "for you strike me as a very intelligent girl. The kind who will grow up to be something quite special."

Blushing to the roots of her hay-colored hair, Dorrie bent to set the little boy on the ground, and after shushing his whimpers at being awakened, she straightened her thin shoulders. "I'll do it."

"Excellent," Matthew said, then he stepped up to the booth, gave the pieman some coins, and requested two pies—one beef, one lamb.

"Here you go," he said, handing the first of the turnovers to Dorrie, "see what you think."

She wasted no time in biting into the flaky crust, sighing with contentment as the warm meat and potatoes slipped down her gullet to her stomach. "Umm," she said.

Blushing again, she asked very softly, "Would yer missus mind, do ye think, sir, if Alfie was to have just a little taste of the pie? I won't let him take but the one bite, I promise. There'll be plenty left for the lady."

Matthew looked from the little girl to the quiet child, who stared hopefully at his sister, and for the first time, Sarah saw something like chagrin upon her employer's face. "The lady would not mind at all," he said, the words not as steady as they had been earlier.

"In fact, you give that pie to the boy while you taste the lamb."

Dorrie broke the turnover into halves and put a half in each of the little boy's hands. Immediately, he began to eat the food in his right hand, not taking his eyes off that in his left. His sister bit into the lamb, chewing slowly, trying to savor the taste. When she stopped at the one bite, Matthew told her to take another.

"See if it is too salty," he instructed.

She bit into the pastry once again, using the back of her hand to wipe the juice that spilled down her chin, then licking the hand. "No, sir. It b'ain't too salty."

"Wonderful," he said. "But what of the meat. Is it tender enough? The lady cannot abide tough meat. Try another bite and give me your opinion."

Only when every morsel had been consumed did Matthew run out of questions as to texture, spice, and the overall delectability of the stuffed pastry. "So," he said when Dorrie wiped her hands on her dress then bent to retrieve her brother, "what is your verdict."

After giving the matter a great deal of thought, she said, "The lamb, sir. I think your missus should try the lamb."

"Excellent," he said, placing a shilling in Dorrie's sticky hand. "You were as good a taster as any in London, and I thank you for your help."

The little girl stared openmouthed at the shiny coin, unable to believe her good fortune; then, with a pride that was as stubborn as it was wonderful, she gave the shilling back to her benefactor. "Best not give me this yet, sir. Not 'til yer missus tries the pie and says if I did the job right."

Sarah looked at Matthew, hopefully conveying to him a silent plea to extricate her from this dilemma. Unfortunately, the gentleman had discovered a pastry crumb on his sleeve and was obliged to employ an undue amount of time to its complete removal. Thus it was that he missed entirely his supposed *wife*'s unspoken appeal to him not to ask this of her.

As the seconds ticked by, and Matthew continued to work on the obstinate crumb, the light of wonder that had shone in Dorrie's large blue eyes at sight of the silver coin began to fade, and suspicious moisture took its place. Not that she cried—she had too much pride for that—but her valiant attempt to stem the tears sliced right through Sarah's heart like a well-honed scythe in a ripe wheat field.

"So," Sarah said, with what enthusiasm she could manage, "the lamb it will be."

Matthew moved with surprising speed, extricating the needed coin from the pocket of his waistcoat, and plunking it down before the pieman. "One lamb turnover, my good man, and see it is the freshest one on your tray."

Queasiness at the thought of what she was about to do forced Sarah to swallow rapidly, and when Matthew brought the still-warm pastry to her and transferred it into her hand, the fatty aroma brought back with an alarming vividness the experience of her childhood. She knew she would never get through this if she did not replace the memory of that experience with a more positive one, and with that object in mind, she thought of the merlin they had seen earlier. Concentrating on the hawk, picturing its beauty and its grace as it soared above the rampart, she took a bite of the meat pie, chewed only long enough to keep the pieces from choking her, then swallowed the whole as quickly as possible.

"What think ye?" Dorrie asked, fairly holding her breath lest the answer be unfavorable. "Will it do, missus?"

Sarah forced a smile to her lips. "I can tell you with complete honesty, little one, that it has been years since I ate anything like it. You did a wonderful job as taster, and I thank you. Now take your shilling, there's a good girl, for the gentleman and I must be going. Immediately."

Sarah did not wait for Matthew but walked with unseemly haste toward the large tent set aside for ladies. Unfortunately, she was still several feet from that rustic retreat, with not so much as a tent peg to hold on to for support, when her stomach rebelled and she cast up her accounts.

Within seconds she heard someone behind her, then strong hands caught her by the shoulders, holding her securely. At that moment she was too busy to ascertain the identity of the Good Samaritan, but it was enough to know that he was there, acting as a shield against onlookers and as a bolster should she feel faint.

"Here," Matthew said, offering her a finely woven linen handkerchief. Sarah took the proffered square and pressed it to her mouth, all the while wishing it was a magician's cloth behind which she might disappear forever. It wanted only this for Matthew Donaldson to see her disgrace herself.

"If you are able to walk now," he said, "I will help you to one of the chairs beneath the awning. Or if you would prefer it, I will find some female to attend you, then I will take myself out of your sight."

"The chair," she said.

When they arrived at the awning and availed themselves of one of the chairs, a middle-aged woman in a crisp white apron and cap stepped from the tent. "May I be of assistance, sir?"

"The lady is unwell," Matthew said. "Bring her a wet cloth, if you please, and a cup of water."

"Yes, sir."

After the attendant untied Sarah's bonnet and set it on a small tea table, she went to do Matthew's bidding. She was back almost immediately with a flannel towel dipped in rose water, and while Sarah placed the cool, wet flannel over her face, then rested her head against the top rail of the chair, the woman went back inside to fetch the cup of water.

"Miss Sterling," Matthew said, "I daresay it would improve your health no end to see me locked in the stocks for dealing you such an underhanded trick. Or perhaps you would prefer I be chased off by a pack of hungry wolves."

"Please," she said, groaning dramatically, "if you have any compassion in your heart, do not say the word 'hungry' within my hearing. Not ever again."

Since her words were accompanied by a quick peek from behind her rosewater mask, Matthew did not resist the temptation to laugh. "Madam," he said, "does this mean you still believe I *have* a heart?"

"Only where *very* young females are concerned. As for the rest of my sex—we with a few more years to our credit—we must take what comfort we can from the knowledge that you cannot sacrifice us *all* before the altar of youth."

The attendant returned with the cup of water, and Sarah drank thirstily. Afterward, she discarded the wet cloth and reached her hands up to her forehead, where dozens of little damp curls framed her face. A tinge of pink showed in her cheeks upon discovering the tendrils. "I . . . I must look a fright."

Matthew shook his head. "Madam," he said, "you quite disappoint me, for I had not thought you one to talk such fustian. If the truth be told, you are quite the loveliest lady I have ever known, and I have been wondering this age why some gentleman has not swept you off your feet and carried you down the aisle."

Chapter Nine

You are quite the loveliest lady I have ever known.

That single phrase traveled around and around inside Sarah's head, with an occasional side trip to her heart; all the while wisdom bade her ignore the entire remark.

Her more logical self advised her to remember that gentlemen who paid compliments with ease had probably had far too much practice in the art, and that too frequent bestowing of accolades cheapened both the praise and the praiser. Still, her more fanciful self mocked the logical, and Sarah hugged the sweet words to her heart—words no man had ever said to her before, and in all likelihood, would never say again.

As for Matthew Donaldson, he neither repeated his compliment nor tried to take it back by pretending it had been said in jest. Having rendered Sarah speechless, he pressed a coin into the attending woman's hand, then asked her to assist Sarah into the tent so she might have a few moments of privacy.

When Sarah stepped back outside a short time later, with her hair arranged neatly beneath her bonnet, and no lingering signs of the malaise that had prompted her to embarrass herself by being ill in public, she found Matthew waiting for her. He had fetched Chloe and Noel, and by common consent, the foursome walked directly to the roped-off area and retrieved the horses. Before very few minutes had passed, Matthew cracked the whip in the air just above the backs of the blood bays, and the team galloped forward, apparently as eager as Sarah to be on the road that led back to Bellingham.

The return drive was uneventful, and as soon as they reached Donmore Hall, her employer insisted that she allow Morag to put her to bed. Though Sarah obeyed the order, appreciative of the thoughtfulness, she felt a complete fraud allowing others to treat her as an invalid when she was perfectly well. To her surprise, her eyelids grew heavy almost as soon as she was beneath the covers, and because she had slept so little the night before, she gave in to a much needed nap.

She came awake with a start when the gong sounded, warning that it was time to dress for dinner. However, before she could quit the bed, the maid returned with a tray bearing a pot of steaming tea, a rack of toast, and a bowl of delicately seasoned vegetable broth.

"The master ordered it," Morag informed her, setting the tray down with care. "Came down to the kitchen himself."

Sarah could not believe her ears. "Mr. Donaldson? In the kitchen?"

"Yes, miss. Fair set the place at sixes and sevens, he did, walking around the room and asking what was for dinner."

"I can well imagine."

"Didn't nobody know what to make of the master coming down like that. The scullery maid, whose a regular idgit if you ask me, hid her face behind her apron and giggled the whole time. Meanwhile, the rest of us just stood about, our mouths open, not knowing what to do or say."

The maid lowered her voice, as if unsure whether or

not she should relate the remainder of her story. "Cook had a good beef broth bubbling on the stove, she did, and though it smelled like a bit of heaven come down to earth, Mr. Donaldson said could she make you sommit without meat.

" 'But Miss likes my beef broth,' Cook told him.

" 'Not today she won't,' he says, so Cook bobbed a curtsy and said she'd be pleased to fix the vegetables."

Flabbergasted at such a show of preferential treatment, and feeling just a bit discomfited at what the staff must be thinking, Sarah asked, "Was that all Mr. Donaldson said?"

Morag looked down at her boots as if finding those mundane objects of genuine interest. "He said you was to stay in bed until morning, miss, and that I was to come tell him if you offered any argument."

Though Sarah felt perfectly fine, she grabbed at that lifeline like a woman drowning in her own embarrassment, for she did not believe she could face Matthew Donaldson at the moment. Surely he must realize that speculation would be rife belowstairs after such an unprecedented visit to the kitchen.

And what if Lady Worthing should hear of it?

Sarah settled once again beneath the covers, more than happy to forego dinner with the guests. Even if her ladyship had not heard about the episode in the kitchen, there was every likelihood she would still be in high dudgeon over the trip to Hadrian's Wall. Without a doubt, she had cherished hopes of a felicitous outcome to that drive—hopes that included Matthew's falling in love with her niece. Having her carefully laid plans thwarted would not make the lady a pleasant dinner companion.

"I have no arguments to offer," Sarah said, "for I believe I shall be quite content to remain in my room."

When Morag began to pour the tea into the cup, she spilled half the contents onto the tray. Hastily grabbing up the napkin and using it to soak up the liquid, she begged Sarah's pardon for the mishap. "I'm that clumsy this evening."

Since the competent young maid was never guilty of such an offense, Sarah asked her what had upset her. "Did Mr. Donaldson say something else while he was in the kitchen?"

"Yes, miss," she replied, blushing all the way up to her mobcap. "The master said for me to come up to the book room, he did. Said he had sommit to say to me in private."

"Oh, dear. No wonder you are flustered. Had you any idea what he wanted?"

The girl shook her head. "I feared I was to get the sack, and my knees was knocking together so fierce I nearly fell half a dozen times before I got to the book room."

Sarah sympathized with that feeling, having been privy to such fears herself. "My dear, had you done anything to warrant being fired?"

"That was what I asked myself. Was sommit broken? Had sommit gone missing? I was that worrit I'd been accused of some crime and was to be thrown out without a reference."

"But you were not," Sarah said, "otherwise you would not be here now."

"No, miss. It was just like Mr. Donaldson had said, he had sommit to ask me."

Civility prohibited Sarah's asking what their employer had wanted, so she waited quietly, hoping Morag would volunteer the information. Though the maid turned even redder than before, and licked her lips as if still unnerved by the summons, she was eager to tell.

"He asked me, Mr. Donaldson did, if I got enough to eat. Me and the rest of the maids. Fair took me by surprise, him asking such a thing of *me*, but he said he thought I was the properest one to ask."

Taking into consideration the two maids from last evening and the little girl that afternoon, Sarah thought she understood Matthew Donaldson's sudden appearance in the kitchen. However, she kept her thoughts to herself. "Do you?' she asked. "Get sufficient to eat, I mean."

"Oh, yes, miss. Cook don't like none of us messing around in the larder and taking food without asking, but she sees there's plenty on our plates at mealtime."

"And you told this to Mr. Donaldson?"

She nodded. "He said if he didn't do nothing else as master of the Hall, he'd see that nobody on the estate went to bed hungry. Then," she said, patting her apron pocket as if to reassure herself that it was not empty, "he give me a shilling and told me not to say nothing about what he had asked."

Her button black eyes grew round as saucers. "Oh, miss. Me and my mouth. I just told it all, didn't I?"

"Never mind," Sarah said, "your secret is safe with me. I shall not mention it to anyone."

Of course, Sarah would not think of going back on her word, but she had to admit that keeping a secret was much easier when there was no one in whom she could confide. Easier still when a person stayed to herself.

For the next eight days following the ill-fated trip to Hadrian's Wall, Matthew Donaldson was absent from the Hall. "Gone to Scotland," Morag had informed her.

With her employer away, Sarah remained apart from the guests, taking all her meals on a tray, either in the gallery or in her bedchamber. She went to the gallery each day except Sunday, and though it rained that Saturday night, turning the roads to mud and making it impossible for the household to attend services that morning, Sarah still observed a day of rest. She chose to remain in her room for a private devotional, then she spent the afternoon writing a letter to her father and reading a book she had borrowed from Matthew Donaldson's library.

Monday she resumed work again, rising early to catch the morning light and not leaving her easel until the light began to fade in the late afternoon. That day she began restoring the first of the paintings, a Vermeer.

She worked quickly, but competently, cleaning the canvas on which two laughing girls sat near a mullioned window, the outlines of their simple blue dresses slightly blurred by the artist. Unfortunately, time and coal fires had discolored the varnish so the blue was not that color preferred by the painstaking Jan Vermeer.

Using a clean wool cloth wrapped around the end of a brush, Sarah applied a light coating of citrus oil as a degreaser; then, she dabbed the still damp canvas very gently with another clean, soft cloth, removing the grime. Once the painting was clean and dry, she assessed those places that needed attention; places where time had loosened the paint or where vermin had weakened the canvas beneath.

The following day she began the actual restoration. She had just finished reattaching a small section of loose paint by filling in the canvas to its surface level with paint she had mixed herself, then reaffixing the original paint over her work, when Chloe Worthing interrupted her.

"Why do you not just fill it in completely with your own paint?" she asked from the doorway.

Sarah had not heard the young lady enter the room, so absorbed was she in her task.

"Would it not be easier to use the new?" Chloe asked.

After setting her brush, tip up, in a tall tin mug, Sarah gave her attention to the visitor. "It would be easier to fill in the whole with the paint I mixed," she agreed, "but the result would be a painting by Jan Vermeer and Sarah Sterling. My objective is to preserve the work of Vermeer. To prolong its life. To restore it to the creator's intent."

She smiled to soften her words. "Just because one *can* do a thing does not mean that doing it would be ethical, or preferable."

The young lady took the rebuke in good part. "Of course," she said. "I spoke without thinking. It is just that the blue you put underneath the loose paint looks identical to the original."

"It is as close as I can make it."

She pointed to the slim, leather-bound book that lay beside her wooden workbox. "My father spent years discovering and recording the formulas used by many of the great masters, mixing and remixing the proportions until he got colors that were nearly indistinguishable from those of the masters. When mixing my paints, I adhere faithfully to my father's formulas."

"How very interesting. I believe I read somewhere that art experts often determined authenticity by the colors. If that is true, I should think some unscrupulous person might find your father's book of great value."

"They might," Sarah agreed, "if they knew of its existence." She took a cleaning cloth and wiped a spot of color from her wrist, purposefully not looking at the young lady. "Until today, I, er, had never told anyone about the book."

Chloe blinked, the point of Sarah's remark clear as crystal. "I understand you, Miss Sterling, and you may rest easy on that head. I am resolved to forget I ever saw it."

Sarah breathed a sigh of relief. "Thank you, Miss Worthing."

"Please. Call me Chloe."

"Chloe," Sarah repeated.

"Actually, I am inordinately pleased that you felt free enough to confide something important to me, for there is a matter upon which I should like your advice."

"Miss Worthing—Chloe—I fear that I would make a poor counselor. I have little experience of the society in which you move."

"Still, you are a woman of intelligence, and just the type of person I should wish to have for a friend."

"Me? Surely you must have other, closer females from whom you might seek advice."

Chloe shook her head. "I have not. My home in Somerset is isolated, offering no females near my age."

"But you just returned from a season in town, did you not?"

She sighed. "Yes, but I made no friends there. I had hoped I might do so. Unfortunately, it did not happen. From the onset of the Season, it became apparent that, because of my looks, the gentlemen were eager to make my acquaintance, while the young ladies were equally eager to keep their distance. Both the sexes judged me entirely upon my appearance, neither bothering to look beneath the surface to the real person."

Having been guilty of that same error, Sarah had the grace to blush. "I had not thought of that."

"No one ever does. No one except—"

She stopped abruptly, as if changing her mind, then she waved a hand as though to brush the subject aside. "I have missed seeing you, Miss Sterling, and—"

"Sarah, please."

The lovely girl was even lovelier when she smiled. "Thank you, Sarah. As I was saying, I have missed your company, and I came in search of you to see if I could persuade you to come down this evening. The meals have been very dull affairs with only Aunt Agatha for company."

"I do not understand. Is Mr. Kemp not with you?"

At the mention of the young man's name, Chloe blushed. "Noel accompanied Mr. Donaldson to Scotland, acting as a sort of guide, to show him the way to his timber holdings. There is a small house there, so they did not plan to return for several days."

Both pieces of information came as a surprise to Sarah; first that Matthew Donaldson owned property other than Donmore Hall, and second that he had chosen Mr. Kemp as his traveling companion.

"I suppose," the young lady said, "that Mr. Donaldson felt it necessary to go to Scotland at this time to escape Aunt Agatha's matchmaking attempts."

Sarah was surprised at such plain speaking. "Does his leaving disappoint you?"

"No. Not at all, for I had no wish to be thrown in his way. Coming to Donmore Hall to make his acquaintance was not my idea."

"Is that because your affections are already settled upon another? Upon Mr. Kemp, perhaps?"

The beauty's mouth fell open. "You knew, then? But, how?"

"I could not help but see the looks that passed between the two of you. If you will forgive my asking, does your family have some serious objection to Mr. Kemp? Though I am no judge of these things, to me he seems a perfectly respectable gentleman."

"Oh, yes, he is most gentlemanly. And so very amiable. And handsome." The young lady sighed. "If only he had inherited the Donmore estate, my family would have had no objections to the match."

Ah, yes. The inheritance. Finance must always play its part in the marriage of true minds. Setting aside her cynicism, Sarah remembered the conversation she had overheard in the breakfast room, a conversation in which Mr. Kemp had urged Chloe to show more fortitude, advising her that she could not be forced to do something she might find abhorrent.

Easy words for a man to say! The case was quite otherwise for a young girl. "Would your parents attempt to force you to marry where you have not given your heart?"

"Oh, no. They are indulgent to a fault. At least, that is what Aunt Agatha says."

"If that is the case, I see no problem. My advice is simple, tell Lady Worthing that you wish to marry Mr. Kemp, then do not let yourself be coerced into going against your principles."

A hint of moisture showed in the girl's big blue eyes. "You do not know Aunt Agatha. She is determined that I shall marry Mr. Donaldson. She wants the property and the collection back in the family."

"Matthew Donaldson *is* family!" Sarah surprised herself and her visitor with her vehemence.

"Yes," Chloe replied, "but he is not a true gentleman, and my aunt believes that I can give him the polish he needs."

White hot anger shot through Sarah, and she was forced to clamp her lips shut to keep from voicing a few well-chosen words concerning Lady Worthing and her overblown estimation of the Donaldson family. Several deep breaths were required before Sarah brought her indignation under control. "Your aunt's opinion notwithstanding, Mr. Matthew Donaldson does not need polishing, for he is a gentleman in the truest sense of the word."

She had no idea why she felt called upon to defend her employer; he was perfectly capable of defending himself if he thought it necessary. He needed no championing by her; still, something in her rebelled at the unfounded assumption that because Matthew had once fallen on hard times, he had abandoned the ethical teachings of his childhood. Did no one take the time to look at the man for who he was? Obviously not. It was much easier to make assumptions and let that conjecture be the basis for judgment.

As it turned out, Sarah did not join the two ladies for dinner that evening, or any evening that week. Using the pressures of her job as an excuse, she availed herself once again of meals served on a tray.

When Sunday dawned dry and beautiful, however, she knew she could not hide behind her work any longer. So it was that she presented herself bright and early that Sabbath morning in the green-and-white breakfast room. To her surprise, the gentlemen had returned sometime during the night, and Matthew Donaldson sat at the head of the rosewood table.

"Good morning," he said, standing politely at her entrance. "I trust I find you well, Miss Sterling."

Unprepared for the encounter, Sarah was momentarily speechless. Odd that in the days he had been away she had forgotten the warmth of his smile, and how it could go directly to a person's heart, rendering that person breathless. "I am quite well, sir. And . . . and you? May one assume you had a pleasant trip?"

Because Chloe chose that moment to enter the room, followed by Mr. Kemp, Matthew's answer, whatever it may have been, was lost in the exchange of greetings. They did not linger over the meal, for the church bells in the village had already begun to peal, and services called. Therefore, within less than twenty minutes the three ladies climbed aboard Mr. Carlton Donaldson's antiquated landau, while the two gentlemen rode the short distance into Bellingham.

The coach wheels rattled over the narrow cobbled streets of the medieval town, past the dozen or so brick and sandstone shops, and beyond the inn yard, stopping before the handsome gray stone church. As before, Sarah's attention was caught by the *pele* built to the rear of the church. After visiting Hadrian's Wall and seeing for herself what the Roman soldiers considered necessary for guarding themselves against attack by the fierce Scottish clans, she could well imagine the villagers of the fourteenth century feeling the need for such a fortification.

After handing the reins of his spirited chestnut to the groom, who jumped down from the box, Matthew helped the ladies from the coach; then, offering his arm to Lady Worthing, he led them down the aisle to the Donaldson pew, which took pride of place at the front of the sanctuary.

As the party made their way to their places, Sarah noticed that Chloe was the recipient of numerous open-mouthed stares from the males in the congregation—a fact that was only to be expected. What came as a bit of a surprise, considering Chloe's own revelation that she had no female friends, was that she also received a smile and a nod from a young lady seated in the pew opposite. Slightly older than the beauty, with locks as blond as Chloe's were dusky, the chit was lively looking rather than pretty, and her appeal owed much to a pair of large green eyes and unusually dark eyelashes.

Obviously surprised to see a familiar face, Chloe was already at the door to the Donaldson pew before she remembered to return the other girl's nod.

"I did not realize," Noel Kemp whispered, "that you were acquainted with anyone in Bellingham."

"Miss Fairlie and I met in town," she replied. "It was her first Season as well, and we were made known to one another at the Queen's drawing room."

The arrival of the acolytes signaled an end to all conversation, so nothing more was said of the young lady until the Donmore party was outside the church, waiting for the arrival of the coachman with the landau.

"What a coincidence your knowing Eve Fairlie," Mr. Kemp said, his handsome face alight with pleasant recollections, "for I have known her for years. She was used to be a rather roly-poly minx, but I see time has worked its magic upon her."

When Chloe made no reply, Sarah took it upon herself to fill the silence that followed. "I assume, sir, that you know the young lady from your many visits to the village when you were a lad."

"Very true. Her older brother, Felix, and I were great friends. Always up to some lark, don't you know, and Eve was as mischievous as her brothers. A great go. Ready for anything, no matter how dangerous. Many's the time Felix and I got up to some adventure not fit for a female, and we were obliged to hide from her to keep her from following us."

As if his recollections summoned her, the young lady appeared before them, a saucy smile on her pert face and her hand outstretched in greeting. "Noel Kemp, you handsome devil, I did not think to see you in Bellingham ever again. When I heard that you had been disinherited, I assumed—"

Receiving a quick nip on the elbow from the plump, middle-aged lady who followed her, the chit stopped midsentence, as if realizing too late the implications of her remark. To cover the faux pas, she turned quickly to Chloe. "And, Miss Worthing. What a surprise to see you here."

"Indeed," said the middle-aged lady, adding her mite to turn attention from her daughter's gaffe, "quite a surprise, for I had no idea you meant to journey to Northumberland. Are you visiting at Donmore Hall?"

Chloe curtsied to Lady Fairlie. "I accompanied my Aunt Agatha, ma'am. She was cousin to Mr. Carlton Donaldson, and she felt it incumbent upon her to pay her respects to the new head of her family."

"Ah, yes," replied the matron, "one must always do one's duty."

Her daughter, obviously bored by talk of duty visits, cast a flirtatious look at Matthew from beneath her dark lashes. "I do not believe I have had the pleasure of your acquaintance, sir."

Matthew bowed and said what was expected of him. "I assure you, ma'am, the pleasure would be all mine."

Ever gracious, Mr. Kemp performed the introductions, beginning with Sarah, but if Lady Fairlie and her daughter were at all impressed to be meeting a female hired to clean and restore the art at Donmore Hall, they hid the fact well.

After giving Sarah the briefest of nods, Miss Eve Fairlie turned a blinding smile upon Matthew, batting her eyelashes and declaring herself charmed to meet him at last. "For I have been longing this age to welcome you to Northumberland."

He returned her smile. "You are very kind, Miss Fairlie. Am I correct in assuming that you are Sir Harold's daughter?"

"Indeed you are," she said with such enthusiasm one might be forgiven for thinking Matthew had guessed a great secret.

Not that Sarah cared. If her employer wanted to encourage the outrageous creature, making a fool of himself into the bargain, it was of no consequence to his art restorer. Let the two of them smile until their faces cracked, and see if *she* took any notice.

"Ooh!" the blond squealed, clapping her hands together in an affected manner that made Sarah blush to be a member of the same sex, "I have a wonderful idea. Today is my brother's birthday, and we are having an informal dinner party to celebrate the occasion. Mostly family, mind you, with just a few of the neighbors, but it should be fun. We would be pleased,

would we not, Mama, if you would come, Mr. Donaldson."

"Quite so," her mama replied.

"Oh, and your visitors, too, of course," Miss Fairlie
said.

That last was added just a bit too slowly to suit
Sarah's notion of genuine hospitality, but after a moment's reflection, she realized that even the delayed
invitation did not include her. She was, after all, not a
visitor, but an employee.

Later that afternoon, she discovered that her employer did not agree with her assessment. "Of course
you were invited," he said. "There can be no two opinions on the subject."

Chapter Ten

They had met quite by accident in the hall, the room from which the house derived its name. It being the Sabbath, Sarah did not even think of going to the gallery, and with time on her hands and strolls alone out-of-doors denied her, she sought to amuse herself and get a bit of exercise by visiting the ancient hall.

Probably Norman in origin, it was a half-timbered apartment that retained much of the formality common to such rooms seven hundred years ago. Dominated by massive tie beams in the center and in the end walls—features quite prevalent during medieval times—it still held the original long, sturdy trestle table upon which the knights and those lesser visitors once ate their meals.

The smaller table was missing from the dais, where the lord and his honored guests once dined, and in its place stood a row of stiff wooden chairs, like sentinels awaiting the return of their leader. Behind the dais and at the far end of the hall stood identical smoke screens.

The original beaten earth floor had been covered over with cobbles two or three centuries earlier, and since Sarah found the cobble floor difficult to traverse in her soft-soled slippers, she chose to examine the artifacts that sat upon the mantelpiece of the huge fireplace. She was engrossed in the scrutiny of a chased silver chalice when Matthew Donaldson spoke her name.

"Oh!" she said, turning instantly. "You gave me quite a start. I thought surely one of the Normans had come back to life and was about to have me flogged for my impertinence in handling his liege's silver."

Matthew chuckled. "The imagination is wont to run a bit wild when one remains overlong in such an imposing place. What say you to a stroll in the west garden? You were there once before, but I doubt you saw much of it."

Knowing he alluded to the morning she had gotten lost in the mist, she chose to ignore the observation; instead, she lifted the hem of her skirt an inch to show him her slippers. "As you see, sir, I am not adequately shod for such an activity."

"A not unusual circumstance for you," he said. "I begin to wonder, Miss Sterling, if you have an aversion to proper footwear."

The sudden memory of their bare feet touching in the darkness outside the attic caused heat to inch its way up Sarah's neck to her cheeks, and she turned her face away lest he see her reaction to the remembered intimacy. "Even if I wore walking boots this very minute," she hurried to say, "there is not time for a stroll in the garden. Not if you mean to accept Miss Fairlie's invitation to dinner."

"Of course," he replied, "I was not thinking. You will wish ample time to dress for the affair."

"*I?*" She turned back to stare at him. "I need no such allowance of time, sir, for I was not invited."

"Do not be absurd. Of course you were."

"You are mistaken. The lady mentioned only you and your visitors, and I am persuaded she would be less than pleased to see me arrive."

"And I should be less than pleased to go without you. You were invited, Miss Sterling, and there can be no two opinions on the subject."

There were two opinions, of course, but as no

amount of argument would change *his*, Sarah was finally obliged to agree. It was either acquiesce or be the
cause of his sending a letter of regret for the entire
Donmore party.

So it was that scarce two hours later, Sarah found
herself being assisted from Mr. Carlton Donaldson's
antiquated landau once again.

Recalling the day of her arrival, when her traveling
companion had obligingly bestowed upon her an un-
ending supply of local gossip, Sarah looked with interest upon the sprawling brick building that was
home to the Fairlies. *Fairlie Park*, the loquacious
woman had confided, *is every bit as pleasant an establishment as Sykes Manor*.

The woman had also included in her commentary
the information that Lady Edwina Camden-Reynolds,
the wife of Mr. John Reynolds of Sykes Manor, was the
only *real* nobility in the neighborhood. Thus, when the
rotund Sir Harold escorted that imposing lady to and
from the dinner table, Sarah was not at all surprised,
for Lady Edwina obviously took precedence in every
house in the environs of Bellingham.

Nor was Sarah's understanding taxed to find
Matthew Donaldson seated on his hostess's right, with
Miss Eve Fairlie to his right. It came as even less of a
surprise when Sarah found herself squeezed in at the
middle of the table, which had been expanded to seat
two-dozen guests, seated between Mr. James Fairlie,
the sixteen-year-old younger son of the house, and
that gentleman's great-uncle, an octogenarian so deaf
his ear trumpet saw almost as much use as his fork.

Later, after Mr. Felix Fairlie had opened his birthday
gifts and the older members of the party had settled
down to games of cards, nothing would do the gentleman's pert sister but that the carpets be rolled back in
the far end of the drawing room so the younger members of the party might amuse themselves in dance.

Miss Abbot, a bespectacled and rather nondescript spinster cousin of Lady Fairlie's, was coerced into playing the pianoforte for the dancers, and without Sarah knowing how it happened, she was elected to turn the pages of the music. Being excluded from the dancing did not bother her so very much, but it vexed her considerably to be relegated to the ranks of the spinsters.

Once the dancing began, a pair of middle-aged matrons drew close to keep an eye on their daughters.

"Such a pity," said one. "The chit would have made him a suitable wife. With her beauty, not to mention a dowry of five thousand pounds, there could have been no objections to the marriage."

"No, indeed," replied her companion. "It would have been an unexceptionable match."

Since the women stood not far from the piano, they were obliged to speak loudly to hear one another above the music; thus, it was impossible for Sarah not to eavesdrop upon their conversation. As well, she had only to look up to see the women reflected in the pier glass that hung between the windows to her right. One of the women was short, with mousy brown hair and a timid air, while the other was a tall matron sporting a gold turban trimmed in yellow grebe feathers. The object of their gossip was Mr. Noel Kemp, who partnered Chloe Worthing.

The turbaned lady sighed. "How different things would have been if only Mr. Kemp had remained the heir to Donmore, for he is always so charming, and his address everything one could wish for in a gentleman. I do not scruple to tell you, Arelia, that I should not have objected to *him* paying his addresses to my Catherine."

"Nor I to my Mary," her mousy friend agreed. "What, I wonder, could have possessed old Mr. Donaldson to cut the young man out of his will? I declare, 'tis all very strange."

"Even stranger than you know, Aurelia, for I had it from my maid, who is cousin to the cook at Donmore Hall, that the old gentleman was not himself that last year. He became suspicious of everyone, though about what I do not know. I do know there was some sort of argument, and just after that he changed his will, disinheriting Mr. Kemp."

Her companion tsk-tsked. "Poor young man."

"But that was only the half of it, for after the funeral, when the new will was read, Carlton Donaldson had failed to mention any of his servants."

The woman gasped. "No provision at all?"

The tall lady shook her head, making the grebe feathers flutter as though still attached to the bird rather than her gold turban. "Some of the servants have been at the Hall for years and years, yet they did not receive so much as a farthing."

At that moment, Miss Eve Fairlie came into view with her partner, Matthew Donaldson, and both the matrons remained silent for a time, watching the couple move through the figures of the dance.

The turbaned lady appeared to be assessing Matthew, a speculative look in her eye, and once the couple progressed to the far end of the line, she gave voice to her opinion. "A handsome enough man."

"Oh, my, yes. Quite handsome."

"Not that I should wish to have him for my Catherine."

"Nor I for my Mary," the mouse replied much too quickly.

"Naturally not. Not a man of his dubious past. Still," she said, almost to herself, "a young lady might fare worse than to become mistress of Donmore Hall."

Her companion chewed her lip as if thinking over what she had just heard. "Much worse," she agreed.

"Which," she added with a sudden show of vitriol, "is what I should imagine the Fairlies had in mind when they invited him to dinner."

"*They* invite him? Pshaw! I would not put it past that hoyden, Eve Fairlie, to have invited him herself. You know how she is once she gets an idea into her head, and if she has decided to have Donaldson, there will be no stopping her."

"Lady Worthing may have something to say to that, for I understand she means to have him for her niece. Which makes me wonder if the young lady fired off as well as her aunt had hoped?"

The turbaned matron gave her companion a disdainful look. "Try not to be more of a fool than you can help, Aurelia. Rumor has it that the lovely Miss Worthing had more than one quite flattering offer. Since the gentlemen were refused, one can only assume the chit wishes to marry for love."

"Mr. Noel Kemp, do you think? He was noticeable in paying his addresses to her during the Season, and he is certainly handsome enough to turn any young lady's head."

"Pshaw. His chances were lost with the loss of Donmore Hall. Mr. Kemp has no recourse now but to marry an heiress." She sighed loudly. "What a pity Donmore Hall was not entailed."

Having come full circle in their conversation, the women were silent for a time, then the turbaned lady asked her companion if she had heard anything of Mr. Matthew Donaldson's preferences. "Is he fond of music, do you know? My Catherine's skill upon the pianoforte is unmatched in the neighborhood. I might get up a musicale."

"I was thinking of that very thing myself, for my Mary has only just learned a charming new piece upon the harp."

The set finally came to an end, prompting the two

matrons to abandon their present spot near the pianoforte to stroll to the other side of the room, where a pair of chairs had just been vacated. Unfortunately, their desertion came too late, for in their wake they left Sarah angry and unaccountably depressed. Though why this should be so, she did not know—or would not admit to knowing.

However, there was one thing she knew for certain, she did not intend to spend another minute turning pages for Miss Abbot. If Sarah was to be excluded from participating in the party, she would do so in private. She would not sit there passively just because others had decided she was "on the shelf."

"If you will excuse me," she said to Miss Abbot, "I should like to take a stroll in the garden before the light fades. I understand the statuary is not to be missed."

Miss Abbot's eyes grew wide behind her spectacles, giving her an owlish look. "The garden? But, Miss Sterling, surely you cannot mean to go out there alone? Not with night coming on." When Sarah declared that was exactly what she meant to do, the lady lowered her voice to a whisper. "But what will people say?"

Sarah was obliged to swallow the rather rude remark that popped into her head. Instead, she said, "They will likely say that I chose a fine evening to view the birdbath."

Considering the discussion at an end, Sarah rose and crossed the room to the French windows that stood open to let in the soft breeze, not stopping until she reached the small landing that gave access to the little enclosed garden. Even though distant clouds were slowly swallowing up the pink and gray of the twilight sky, still she could see that it was a charming spot.

Aside from one rather handsome marble Cupid that

took pride of place at the rear of the garden, the statues were mostly uninspiring renditions of woodland creatures; however, their charm came not from their artistic merit but from their artless positioning. Each creature had been placed within a planting of shrubs or a bed of unpretentious plants such as sweet cicely or lady's mantle, and they looked surprisingly natural, as though they had paused for only a moment to enjoy the peacefulness of the garden.

The effect was delightful.

A gravel walk led to the Cupid and a small, wrought-iron settee, and Sarah decided upon that as her destination. She had only just arrived at the statue when she felt someone watching her. When she turned and looked, Matthew Donaldson was on the landing. He stood quite still, his attention fixed on her, and though his expression was unreadable at the distance, Sarah had the oddest feeling that he was annoyed.

With no place to go, she disposed herself upon the little iron settee and waited while Matthew walked toward her, his long strides bringing him there in a matter of seconds. He was definitely annoyed.

"I was looking for you," he said without preamble. "Why did you leave the party?"

She chose not to dissemble. "I was not enjoying it."

"No more was I," he said.

"I find that hard to believe, sir, especially with the vivacious Miss Fairlie applying herself to the task of entertaining you."

The moment the words left her mouth, Sarah wished she could call them back. She could not believe she had uttered such a remark, for even to her own ears it sounded old-cattish, as though she were jealous of the young lady.

If Matthew noticed, he said nothing. Without being invited to do so, he sat down beside her, stretching his long legs out in front of him and crossing one ankle over the other, for all the world as though he and she were old friends, and he could relax in her company. "That is why I came looking for you. I found the young lady's vivacity a bit wearying."

"Wearying? Surely such an assessment is a bit harsh, sir."

"Perhaps, but a fellow cannot remain overlong in the company of females who are trying to set their caps at him without feeling a desire to take himself off."

"Set their caps at you? You are very forthright this evening, Matthew Donaldson. What if you are mistaken?"

He gave her a sidelong look. "Madam, I only wish I were mistaken."

"This is plain speaking indeed. May I ask, sir, if the word *coxcomb* means anything to you?"

The corners of his mouth twitched, but he chose not to answer her question. "Should I pretend that I am not being pursued? Perhaps I will give less offense, Miss Sterling, if I tell you that I do not blame them for their pursuit. Not unlike men, women must be clothed and fed, and marriage is the conventional way for ladies to achieve that goal. I take no umbrage with females wishing to marry well."

"A very tolerant view, sir. On behalf of females the world over, pray allow me to thank you for your understanding."

He chuckled. "Madam, I am a very understanding fellow."

"And so modest."

"That, too, for I have much to be modest about."

This time it was Sarah who chuckled. "As your employee, perhaps I would be wise not to comment upon that observation."

When the muted strains of a waltz drifted through the open French windows, Matthew stood and held his hand out to Sarah. "Come," he said, "you owe me a dance."

Though waltzing with him was exactly what she wanted to do, she hesitated. "How does it happen, sir, that I owe you anything?"

"During that interminable set with the endlessly vivacious Miss Fairlie, I kept watching you sitting beside the pianoforte, calmly turning the pages, and all I could think of was how pleasant it would be to dance with a lady with a modicum of intelligence."

"A modicum? Sir, you are too kind."

"And you are a minx. But do not let us split hairs, madam, for you cannot be unaware of my respect for your intellect."

While Sarah basked in the glow of this unlooked-for compliment, he continued. "I promised myself the pleasure of the next set with you, but before I could claim my dance, you vanished. It was while I searched for you that I was cornered by a very imposing matron in a feathered turban. Since my escape from the woman was contingent upon my agreeing to attend some blasted musicale at her home, I have laid the entire fault at your door. Ergo, you owe me some sort of recompense."

Without another word, he caught her hand and pulled her to her feet, but when he would have placed his hand at her waist, she reminded him that they stood upon a gravel walk. "We cannot dance here, for I am wearing slippers."

"I might have known," he said, "for you have a predilection for inappropriate footwear."

"I protest, sir, for how was I to know you liked to dance upon gravel? Of course, had I known of *your* predilection for unusual surfaces, I would have ignored the conventions and worn boots to Lady Fairlie's dinner party."

As Matthew looked into her upturned face, her

brown eyes were alight with teasing laughter and her mouth quivered from the attempt to contain the smile that begged to be released. Her eyes were beautiful, but it was that quivering mouth that held his attention and shot a bolt of lightning through his veins. His gaze focused upon her soft lips, and it was all he could do not to gather her in his arms and cover her mouth with his own.

"I give you fair warning, minx. Forsake your saucy ways, or I shall be forced to do something we might both regret."

"And what might that be, sir? Oblige me to dance barefoot on a bed of nails?"

"Madam," he said, tugging at her hand to bring her a step closer, "I warned you."

He would have kissed her that very moment if a genuine bolt of lightning had not lit up the heavens, followed by a boom of thunder that shook the earth and prompted Sarah to grasp his hand tightly. "Oh, dear," she said, looking toward the ever-darkening sky, "it appears our dance will have to wait. Unless, of course, you enjoy being caught in thunderstorms."

She had no more than uttered the words when the sky opened up, pouring gallons of water on their heads, and though Matthew held on to her hand, helping her to run, her dress was soaked through before they reached the end of the garden path. When they arrived at the French windows, they found Mr. Kemp looking for them.

"There you are," he said. "Lady Worthing wishes to leave for the Hall immediately, before the roads become quagmires."

"By all means," Matthew agreed. "While I procure a wrap for Miss Sterling, I shall leave it to you to call for the landau and the horses. And without delay, cousin, lest we become stranded and are obliged to call upon the Fairlies' hospitality overnight."

Though his tone had sounded sincere, Sarah dared not look at him, for she knew, if Mr. Kemp did not, that Matthew Donaldson was exercising his *predilection* for sarcasm.

The landau was called for, and by the time the party reached Donmore Hall, the rain had turned into a deluge worthy of the name. Because the gentlemen had traveled by horseback, they looked as though they had taken spills into a river.

"Take my advice, Donaldson," Lady Worthing instructed as they parted at the head of the stairs—she, her niece, and Mr. Kemp going to the right, toward the west wing, while Sarah and Matthew went left, toward the east wing—"have your man make you a tisane of bittersweet and ling liver oil. And drink it hot!"

Her parting words were for Sarah, who was engulfed in one of Mr. James Fairlie's outgrown woolen greatcoats. "As for you, Miss Sterling, I advise dosing with pennyroyal, else you will surely have a putrid throat by morning."

"Yes, ma'am," Sarah replied demurely, though as soon as the other three disappeared down the corridor, she burst out laughing.

"Easy for you to laugh," Matthew said, pausing at the corridor that led to the yellow bedchamber. "You are advised to take mint tea, while I have been instructed to partake of herbs and rotted liver."

"And shall you do it, sir?"

"If I said I should rather dance barefoot on a bed of nails, would you then refuse the pennyroyal? I should not like my art restorer to become ill."

A serious note in his voice stilled her laughter. "Sir, I never catch cold."

To her dismay, he caught the lapels of the greatcoat, one in either hand, then he slowly drew her toward him until they were mere inches apart. "Humor me," he said softly, "and drink the tea."

Because their nearness robbed her of speech, she merely nodded her head.

"Good girl," he whispered, then he bent his head and brushed his lips across hers with a gentleness that left her knees almost too weak to support her.

Without another word, he turned and walked toward the front of the house.

He had rounded the corner of the corridor that led to the master bedroom and the gallery before Sarah recovered the use of her legs. However, she did not go immediately to the door of the yellow bedchamber. Knowing that Morag waited for her inside the chamber, she lingered a moment longer, wanting a bit of privacy. Then she lifted her fingertips to her mouth, touching the still-tingling spot where Matthew's lips had been.

Chapter Eleven

Sarah did not have a good night, though her sleeplessness had nothing to do with her having been soaked by the rain, and everything to do with the memory of Matthew's lips, warm and firm upon hers. To honor his request, she had allowed Morag to prepare a cup of tea with pennyroyal, and after drinking every drop, Sarah had climbed into bed and snuggled beneath the warm covers.

But sleep had not come. Too much was going on inside her brain.

Why was it, she had asked herself a hundred times, that she would rather stand in the rain with Matthew Donaldson than bask in the sun with any other man she had ever met? Or climb to the top of an ancient Roman wall? Or follow a trail to a waterfall?

To each of those questions, the same answer offered itself, though Sarah emphatically refused to accept the explanation. She was not in love with Matthew! She could not—would not—allow herself to be. She would not travel down that road, for that way led only to heartbreak.

Matthew Donaldson might tease her; he might treat her as a friend, a confidant; he might even kiss her; but when it came time to wed, he would choose one of those young ladies who had set their caps at him. He would marry a girl with the proper background—a girl accustomed to moving in the first circles. One whose wealth would join with his; one whose youth and beauty would proclaim her a diamond of the first water.

He would not choose his art restorer. He would not align himself with Sarah Sterling.

She tossed and turned and bid herself put Matthew from her mind, but all to no avail. He would not leave her thoughts.

How foolish she had been after the incident outside the attic door. She knew then that she was attracted to her employer, but she had told herself that if she was never alone with him except when in broad daylight, and that if she did not get near enough to him to smell that spicy masculine scent that clung to his skin, she would be in no danger of succumbing to temptation. If only she would not act foolishly and reach out to touch him, she would be safe, in no danger of losing her heart.

Stay away. Do not touch him. How easy those words were to say, and how difficult they had been to obey. She had done everything she had vowed not to do, and now she loved him.

Unable to endure her own thoughts another minute, Sarah rose and dressed, donning a freshly laundered apron. Light was only just showing at the edges of the window hangings, but she decided to go to the gallery even so. She needed to work. Idleness was no friend. If she labored long enough and hard enough, perhaps she might work through the worst of her emotional turmoil.

Having risen even before the maid, Sarah tiptoed about the bedchamber. After taking the slim leather-bound book of formulas from the drawer of the dressing table and slipping it into the pocket of her apron, she found her workbox and silently quit the room.

She met no one in the corridor, and once she was inside the gallery, with the door shut behind her, she felt more herself. The smell of fresh paints, the sight of brushes standing upside down in a jar, those were things she knew and understood—familiar things— with them, she knew her worth. They were her tools; she treated them with respect and they never disappointed her. They never broke her heart by choosing another.

The first rays of the sun showed through the windows of the gallery, and though the light was not sufficient to allow Sarah to work on one of the canvases to be restored, it was sufficient to allow her to walk about the room. She was coming to know these beautiful paintings, and as she strolled the length of the gallery, she paused before a few of her favorites. She had just stopped before a Rubens and was headed toward a landscape by John Constable that she found particularly calming, when she felt an uneasiness.

Something was wrong. What, she could not really say. Everything seemed all right, nothing was missing, yet something nagged at her, a fleeting impression garnered in passing.

Going back to the deal worktable, she lit a brace of candles then followed the same route she had taken moments ago, holding the candles aloft beside each picture. There was the Rubens, in need of cleaning, but otherwise intact. Beside that hung a Van Dyck, and to the right of the Van Dyck was Hans Eworth's portrait of the young boatman in the blue tasseled cap.

As she gazed at the boatman, Sarah's stomach tightened into a knot. She held the candles higher, hoping the shadows had fooled her. They had not. This was not the portrait she had inventoried several days ago. The Flemish master never painted this picture!

Outrage and fear warred for dominance inside Sarah, and as she stared at the abomination on the wall, she knew she had to tell Matthew. The paintings were left to him—as a trust, he had said—and he must be apprised of the theft immediately.

She had no way of knowing when the paintings were switched, it could have been only minutes before she came to the gallery; if so, the thief might be close by. They might catch him before he could flee. With this thought in mind, she tiptoed across the corridor to the master bedroom, and knocked softly upon the door. No one answered.

Knowing this was too important a matter to let herself be ruled by the conventions, she opened the door and stepped inside the room. "Matthew," she called. When he did not answer, she crossed the thick carpet to stand beside the large, full tester bed where Matthew Donaldson lay sleeping. He had flung one arm outside the covers, while the other was tucked firmly beneath the pillow, and in the soft light he appeared almost vulnerable. A lock of hair had fallen across his forehead, and it was all Sarah could do not to reach out and brush the dark brown strands back from his face.

"Matthew," she called again. When he did not answer this time, she tapped him on the shoulder.

He opened his eyes only partially, and when he saw her he smiled. "Sarah," he murmured, his voice hoarse with sleep. "Sweet Sarah."

"Matthew," she said, "wake up. I need you."

He came awake instantly, his eyes open wide, and he stared at her as if unable to believe what he saw. "Damnation, Sarah!" he said. "What the deuce are you doing here?"

Matthew had not enjoyed a restful night. After he had brushed his lips against Sarah's then walked away, he had come to his bedchamber and prepared for bed. He had downed a glass of brandy to help ward off the chill, then a second glass to help get his mind off his lovely art restorer. And though he was slightly bosky, sleep would not come.

Images of Sarah kept intruding upon his thoughts. Sarah at the pianoforte, turning the pages of the music and looking regal as a queen. Sarah in the garden, sitting on the wrought-iron bench in the sweet-scented twilight, watching him as he came to her. Sarah, looking like an adorable waif in young Fairlie's greatcoat. Her laugh, her smile, her voice, they had all conspired to keep him awake.

When he had taken her by the lapels, and she had let him pull her close, he had ached to hold her in his arms and kiss her; not that brief touch he had allowed himself—sweet though it was—but a real kiss. The wanting had been even worse than that night outside the attic—and that had been sheer hell!—especially when she had put her hand on his chest, and her gentle fingers had touched the bare skin at his throat.

Lately, it seemed that wanting to kiss Sarah was taking up an inordinate amount of his time, and he had no idea what to do with his frustration. He wanted her, yet he knew he could not bed her as he usually would do with the kind of women he had known in the past. Sarah was a lady, and she deserved a gentleman, a man of refinement, not a soldier of the line who had seen his share of life's harsh realities.

When he first opened his eyes and saw her standing beside his bed, he thought she was part of a dream— or perhaps a dream come true. Then she had spoken his name and he had been shocked awake, unable to believe that she had come to him.

It took his drink-befuddled brain a moment to assimilate that she had said she needed him.

"The thief," she said, her voice just above a whisper, "he has switched one of the pictures in the gallery."

                    *   *   *

Matthew looked at the portrait of the boatman. "How can you be certain?"

"Everything is wrong. Not only is the rich texture of Hans Eworth's painting missing, but the colors are also flat and not quite true. Actually, this is not even a good forgery. It is more like a copy an amateur might execute merely for the pleasure of doing it."

The words had no more than left her mouth when she groaned. "The attic," she said, then she turned and sped from the room.

Matthew had not stopped to dress before leaving his bedchamber, contenting himself with grabbing his dressing gown and the pistol from his bedside table. Now, however, he wished he had taken a moment to don his boots. He had no idea why Sarah had run from the room, nor what the attic had to do with anything, but since he dared not let her out of his sight—not if she was right about the pictures being switched—he had, perforce, to follow her.

Even barefoot he could outrun her, so he caught up with her long before she reached the top floor. "What is this about?" he asked, catching her arm and halting her progress.

"That painting, the one now hanging in the gallery, I believe I saw it in the attic."

He held her arm until she agreed to let him step in front of her, then he preceded her down the narrow, uncarpeted corridor. The plank steps rebelled at bearing his weight, squeaking so loudly they would have given ample warning should anyone be hiding behind the door, so he raised his pistol before lifting the latch.

"There is a dressmaker's dummy," Sarah warned him, but if the scowl on his face was anything to go by, he did not appreciate the information.

"Shh," he said.

The attic was as covered in cobwebs as it had been when Sarah had seen it last, and the smell of camphor still permeated the air, but the only humans in the dusty place were she and Matthew. Even the pan-niered dummy with its moth-eaten peruke had been moved to a far corner.

"Over there," she said, pointing to the wall where she had left the amateur canvases stacked. Skirting the wobbly table where she had set her candle the last time she was there, and ignoring the two water-stained old sea chests, she moved over to the wall.

Someone had been there all right, and not just to re-locate the lady in the panniers, for the gilt-framed pic-tures were stacked neatly in one spot, while the other dozen and a half unframed canvases had been dis-carded, tossed aside like so much rubbish. Quickly, Sarah looked through the lot. "It is not here," she said.

"What, if I may ask, is not here?"

"A copy of the boatman. I saw it when I was here be-fore, and now it is gone. Though I do not think it has gone very far."

"What are you saying?"

"I am saying that someone discovered the copy, and while we were away from the Hall, he—or she—switched it for the original."

"You are certain?"

"Quite," she said. "The copy is downstairs, hanging in the gallery. Where the real portrait may be, I cannot say."

The thefts could be kept quiet no longer. Now that there was no doubt whatsoever that someone was re-moving paintings, Matthew decided to hire a pair of Bow Street runners, one to come to Donmore Hall, the other to see what he could discover there in London about the man in the mist and his employer, Mr. Way-ford. When the letter to Bow Street was written, re-questing the services of the robin redbreasts—a sobriquet given the detectives because of their conspicuous red waistcoats—Matthew called for his horse to be saddled and brought around.

"Do you recall the man we heard talking that day you were lost in the mist?" he asked Sarah when he came to the gallery to tell her he was bound for the village.

At the recollection, she felt a shiver run up her spine. "Of course I remember. How could I forget? The Cockney told the other person—the one I never heard speak—to be in London within a fortnight, with the promised goods, or he would be back."

"And if he was obliged to return," Matthew continued, "the Cockney threatened that it would be that other person's last day this side of hell."

"Yes, I recall that as well. Why do you ask?"

"Because the fortnight ends tomorrow, and if our thief has not got enough 'goods' to satisfy the mysterious Mr. Wayford, he may strike again. That is why I am headed for Bellingham to fetch the blacksmith. Before the sun sets on this day, I want a key to the gallery door. To accomplish that end, I mean to bring the smithy back with me, even if I am obliged to drag him here at gunpoint."

Sarah was in complete agreement with Matthew's goal, if not his proposed tactics.

"And I hope I do not have to remind you, madam, not to do anything foolish, like walking about the grounds, or investigating secluded parts of the house."

She took his reminder in good part. "I will remain here, with the footman standing guard just outside the door, until you return."

"Good girl," he said, then he turned and strode from the room.

It was while Sarah stood at the gallery window, watching Matthew astride the spirited chestnut he had ridden the first time she had ever seen him—the day

he and she brought the stagecoach into the village—
that the first of her visitors arrived.

"Miss Sterling," Lady Worthing said, "what is this I
hear about a painting being stolen, and a copy being
left in its place?"

Reluctantly, Sarah turned from watching Matthew
and the gelding as they galloped up the meandering
carriageway then disappeared behind the stand of oak
trees. "It is the picture just there," she said, pointing to
the copy of the boatman, which had been removed
from the wall and was now propped against a leg of
the deal worktable. "I discovered the substitution
quite early this morning."

Lady Worthing moved closer to the painting, studying it with intensity, her lips pursed so tightly the
black silk patch at the corner of her mouth threatened
to come unpasted. "You are quite certain? There can
be no mistake?"

Disinclined to justify her evaluation, Sarah said
only, "I am certain."

"Well," said her ladyship, "this is most distressing
news. Indeed, most distressing, for the collection has
been in the family for years."

The older lady's face looked rather wan beneath the
rouged cheeks and the layer of powder, and Sarah felt
a moment's pity for her. "I am sorry, ma'am."

"Naturally," Lady Worthing continued, as though
Sarah had not spoken, "I might have guessed how it
would be, with such a one made heir to Donmore."

Sarah gasped. With the shock of discovering the
theft of the Eworth portrait, plus the additional stress
of having gotten very little sleep the night before, her
emotions were raw, and she was unable to contain her
anger. "You may be interested to know, Lady Worthing, that other artwork is missing."

"Other paintings? What are you saying?"

"I am saying that Matthew has reason to believe the

thefts began around the time of Mr. Carlton Donaldson's final illness. In fact, it is more than likely that the old gentleman discovered the thievery shortly before his death."

It was her ladyship's turn to gasp. "But how . . . who . . ." She paused, and after a moment of stunned silence, she gasped again. "Oh, good heavens!"

It was obvious that Lady Worthing had never learned to play loo, or any other card game requiring an unreadable expression, for her face revealed unalloyed dismay. "It is Noel," she said, much like a judge pronouncing sentence. "Noel Kemp is the thief."

"No!" someone shouted from the doorway.

Sarah turned in time to see Chloe Worthing, her lovely eyes wide with astonishment. "Aunt! How can you even think such a thing?"

" 'Tis obvious, my dear, it can be none other than he. Only consider, if you will, Carlton's sudden decision to disinherit Noel after years of allowing the lad to live upon the expectation of being heir."

"That proves nothing," Chloe said.

"If you need further proof, there is the argument between the two of them just before Carlton's death. Noel may say it was but a misunderstanding, but I say a gentleman is not banished from a house without serious provocation." Her ladyship tsk-tsked. "Noel Kemp a thief. Who would have thought it?"

"Noel is not a thief!" Chloe all but shouted, "and I forbid you to say he is."

Lady Worthing's mouth fell open, and she stared at her niece. If a kitten had suddenly turned to a ferocious lion before her ladyship's very eyes, she could not have been more surprised. "You forbid? Remember to whom you are speaking, my girl. I am not accustomed to such rudeness, and I can only assume you have taken leave of your senses."

"To the contrary, Aunt. I believe I have just found them."

Sarah wished she were anyplace but there, witnessing Chloe's mental coming of age. "If you will excuse me," she said, backing away from the Worthing ladies, "I must speak with Morag about something."

"Please stay," Chloe said. "For I am doing no more than Noel—and you—advised me to do. I am taking control of my own life. From this point on, I refuse to let others convince me that they know better than I what I should do, and whom I should love."

The young lady turned to her aunt. "I should not have let you bring me to Donmore Hall. And once here, I should not have stayed. It must be obvious, even to the most optimistic matchmaker, that Mr. Donaldson has no interest in marrying me. And I definitely do not wish to marry him."

"Not marry him!" her ladyship said, all else forgotten. "What nonsense is this? I see you are overwrought, my dear, and who can blame you with all this talk of thieves. Therefore, we will not speak of the matter again until later, when you have had sufficient time to think. Perhaps a short rest upon your bed will aid you to see where your best interest—"

"You are correct, Aunt Agatha, I am overwrought, but if I should lie upon my bed for a twelve-month, I should not change my mind about marrying Mr. Donaldson. I love Noel Kemp, and if he will have me, I mean to become his wife."

It was not to be marveled at that Lady Worthing found this pronouncement difficult to countenance, so after trying one more argument, and getting nowhere with her obstinate niece, she warned the young lady that her parents would hear of this foolishness. "I shall write to your father immediately, and we will see what he has to say about your throwing away an opportunity of a lifetime."

Once her ladyship had quit the room, Chloe turned to face Sarah. "Noel is innocent," she said. "I hope you believe me."

"Lady Worthing's observations concerning the cause for the argument between Mr. Kemp and Mr. Carlton Donaldson seem logical, as does her conclusion that he was disinherited when Old Mr. Donaldson discovered him to be a thief."

"But he is not a—"

"Even so, I cannot convince myself that Mr. Kemp had anything to do with the missing pictures."

"Oh, thank you," Chloe said, throwing her arms around Sarah's neck and hugging her. "I knew I had found a friend in you."

Slightly embarrassed by the young lady's exuberance, Sarah asked her if she had seen Mr. Kemp this morning.

"No," Chloe said, going to stand beside the window, "but I spoke to him through his bedroom door."

At Sarah's astonished stare, Chloe related that the young gentleman was remaining abed that morning. "He hopes to ward off what feels like the onset of a cold. The rain last evening," she said, by way of explanation.

"I assume," Sarah said, unable to stop herself, "that he did not heed Lady Worthing's advice about that tisane of bittersweet and ling liver oil."

The two young ladies were still laughing when Bailey scratched at the door and asked Sarah if she would please come look at a painting that had been found in one of the maids' sleeping rooms.

"At Mr. Donaldson's request, miss, we are making a thorough search of the Hall, from roof to cellar, and what should we find right off the mark but a miniature, all wrapped up in a square of velvet. Not knowing but what it might be very old, I decided not to touch it until you had had a chance to examine it."

Sarah agreed to accompany the butler, but she asked Chloe if she would mind waiting for her. "I cannot work today, and I do not care to be alone."

Chloe readily agreed to wait, and while Sarah and Bailey were gone, Angus Newsome visited the gallery. Bowing to Chloe, he told her he had heard of the theft and had come to see if he could be of any assistance.

"Is that the painting, miss?" he asked, pointing to the copy stacked against the table leg.

"It is *not*," she said. "That, of course, is the problem. Although I understand it is quite like the original."

The steward took an inordinate amount of time looking at the framed canvas, studying it from several angles. "It looks quite nice to me," he said. "Not that I know aught of painting. Still, I wonder how Miss Sterling can be so certain it is a copy."

"I believe she could tell by the color."

The man lifted his eyebrows, skepticism evident in the gesture.

Having defended her beloved earlier, the young lady decided she must champion her new friend as well. "Miss Sterling knows all about colors," she said. "Down to the very formulas that each master used in his work."

"Begging you pardon, miss, but no one knows that much."

Chloe stuck our her pretty chin defiantly. "Sarah does. And she never makes a mistake, because she has a book with all the formulas written in it."

Chapter Twelve

"And was it a miniature from the Donaldson collection?" Noel Kemp asked.

He and Matthew were in the book room, enjoying a simple tea of Bohea and shortbread, though there was a dram of something a bit stronger in Mr. Kemp's tea, to help ward off the cold he insisted he had not contracted.

"It was, indeed, a miniature," Matthew replied, "but not one from the collection. Actually, it was one of those profile silhouettes cut from black paper and pasted onto a white pasteboard. The kind a person may have done for twopence at any country fair. I believe it was a likeness of the maid's mother."

They both laughed, but Noel said he thought Bailey had done the right thing in calling Sarah. "After all, it might have been valuable."

"And fragile," Matthew said, setting his cup in its saucer and placing them both on the edge of the oak desk, beside the thick metal key the blacksmith had just had delivered.

"One of the things that bothers me most about this latest theft," Matthew said, "is the fragility of the piece itself. Whoever removed the Hans Eworth portrait from the frame, to replace it with the copy, risked doing irreparable damage to the two-hundred-and-fifty-year-old canvas. And where is the canvas now?

Does the thief have any idea how to handle such a delicate piece?"

Matthew slammed his fist against the side of the desk. "Damnation! If the canvas is mishandled, it may be lost not only to the collection, but also to the world."

"By Jove," Mr. Kemp said, "that would be a travesty, a real—" His comment was interrupted by a bout of coughing, following by a judicious swallow of tea. "Sorry," he said.

"Perhaps you should return to your bed. Surely the business matter you wished to discuss with me can wait."

"Actually, I should like to present my proposal now, so you can be considering it."

"As you wish."

Noel drew his chair up to the other side of the desk, then he removed a sheet of velum from inside his coat, unfolded the paper, and handed it across to Matthew. "That is a faithful listing of all my assets," he said. "I own a modest town house on Chesterfield Street, a phaeton and pair, four hunters—I ride with the Quorn, don't you know—and I have about fifteen thousand invested in the Exchange."

Looking up from the sheet, Matthew said, "Though I find this all quite interesting, I fail to see why you wished me to know of it. Should you not, perhaps, be presenting this information to Miss Worthing's father? You do mean to ask for her hand, do you not?"

"That is my ultimate goal, but first I wanted you to understand that being disinherited by Cousin Carlton did not render me a pauper. It was a facer, that I readily admit, but I was never down for the count. And even had I been, it would not have induced me to embrace a life of thievery."

"I never thought it would," Matthew replied quietly.

Relaxing somewhat at that assurance, Noel continued. "I was left some money by my paternal grand-
mother, so I have enough for a comfortable, if not
extravagant, life. What I need, before asking Chloe to
join her life with mine, is a home."

He was obliged to take a sip of the fortified tea before continuing. "I hoped you might lease me the
property in Scotland. It has suffered from having an
absentee landlord, and I am persuaded that if it was
managed properly, it could be made profitable for
both you and me. As well, cousin," he added with a
grin, "allowing me to lease the place would keep it in
the family."

After the hectic day they had experienced, everyone
at the Hall—master, visitors, and servants alike—
agreed to the wisdom of a simple supper and an early
bed. The decision suited Sarah quite well, for she was
exhausted, especially since she had slept little the
night before. She had already climbed beneath the
covers and was about to blow out the candle on her
bedside table when someone knocked at her bedchamber door.

Morag had just entered the dressing room, bound
for her cot, but she turned at the sound. "You want I
should get that, miss?"

"Please," Sarah replied, already half asleep.

The maid hurried to the door, but when she opened
it just a crack, no one was there. However, on the floor,
next to the threshold, sat a tray containing a pot of tea
and two cups.

"Ooh, miss," she said, lifting the tray and bringing it
inside the bedchamber, " 'tis a nice pot of tea. Just
what you need to help you rest."

Though Sarah doubted anything could keep her
awake tonight, she sat up. "How thoughtful. Did you
request it, Morag?"

"No, miss." She sniffed at the spout. "But it be more pennyroyal, just like last night, so I'll wager the master had it sent up. You want I should pour you sommit while it's nice and hot?"

"Yes, please. And one for yourself, for I imagine you are as upset by this stealing business as the rest of us."

Morag poured the two cups, set Sarah's on the bedside table, then bobbed a curtsy and took her own cup to the dressing room. "Good night, miss," she said, then she shut the connecting door.

Sarah took only a few sips of the pungent liquid, just enough to be able to tell Matthew she had not spurned his thoughtful gift, then she set the half empty cup back on the table. She was asleep within a matter of minutes.

Much later that night, Sarah heard someone moving about in her room. Assuming that some new treachery had occurred, and that Morag had come to wake her, Sarah tried to open her eyes. Oddly enough, her lids would not cooperate. They felt abnormally heavy, and they kept falling shut, giving her only a shadowy impression of someone standing near the dressing table. As well, when she tried to speak, nothing came out but a feeble croaking sound.

Feeble as the sound was, the shadow person must have heard it, for he turned quickly, knocking something onto the floor in his haste.

Some primal instinct warned Sarah of danger, and she blinked several times trying to bring her vision into focus. "M'rag . . ." she called, but the word came out not as a shout but as a whimper, slurred and slow, and echoing as though she were in a deep hole.

Her mouth was so dry she could not swallow, her temples pounded like thunder, and her pulse raced, and all she could do was pray she would wake soon, for this was a nightmare come to life. Someone was in her room and she was powerless to do anything about it; she could neither run nor call for help.

Held by some lethargy she did not understand, Sarah lay there, waiting for what would happen. It happened faster than she could have imagined, for like some creature out of one of those Gothic horror tales from the Minerva Press, the shadow person suddenly dashed toward the bed. While Sarah tried to lift her arms to defend herself, he snatched the pillow from beneath her head and placed it over her face.

Air! She needed air! She could not breathe, and though she tried to turn her head, to fight for her very life, she was too weak. And the shadow person was like a demon, strong and determined to prevail. Cruel and uncaring, he pressed the pillow down tighter and tighter, never relenting, until Sarah thought her lungs would burst from the pain of deprivation.

When she could struggle no longer, and went limp as a child's rag doll, the demon relaxed his hold. By that time, however, she had already begun to float away into blessed oblivion.

"Sarah," called a voice from far, far away. "Sarah, can you hear me?"

She knew that voice. She liked it. It was deep and rich, and at the moment, a bit frantic. It was Matthew's voice, and he wanted her to do something. Any other time she would have been happy to do anything he asked, but at that moment she was too tired.

"Sarah," he called again, "wake up. Please." After having asked her so politely, he ruined the whole by slapping her face, first one cheek and then the other.

Stop that! she wanted to say. *It stings.*

He was also slapping her hands and her feet. No. That could not be right. To slap all those places at once, he would have to be one of those tentacled crea- tures from the ocean. What were they called, those creatures? She could not seem to recall the name, and somehow it seemed very important that she do so.

"Matth . . ." she began, then was obliged to swallow. "What is it called?"

She heard something that sounded like a groan, then she felt strong arms go around her shoulders, lifting her, and pulling her gently against an amazingly comforting chest.

"Matthew?" she said, the word still not very loud.

"I am here," he answered.

"What is that thing with all the arms? I mean tentacles?"

"She is delirious," someone said from quite close by.

Surprised to hear another voice, Sarah forced her eyes open. The speaker was Lady Worthing, and she stood at the foot of Sarah's bed. She was not dressed, but wore a rather youthful lace-trimmed wrapper and a nightcap tied beneath her chin. Her face was naked of rouge, powder, and patch, and she looked frightened.

Frightened? What foolishness. Why should Lady Worthing be . . .

With the force of a galloping horse, last night's horror came back to Sarah, and she began to shake. When Matthew's arms tightened around her, she turned her face into his shoulder. "I could not breathe," she said. "A . . . a shadow, held something over my face. Pushed hard. I tried to fight . . . wanted to fight . . . my arms did not work."

"You were drugged," Matthew said, and though he spoke softly, there was anger in his voice. Raw, barely contained anger. "And what you saw was not a shadow, but a flesh-and-blood man." He muttered something beneath his breath. "If I find the bastard, I will throttle him with my own hands, and we will see how he likes such treatment."

Sarah heard a knock at the door, then Chloe was saying something about a doctor.

"Good man," Matthew said. "I thank you for coming so quickly."

He had been sitting on the edge of Sarah's bed, but now he laid her back against her pillows, his movements so gentle one would have thought she was a porcelain doll. Then he stood and stepped aside so the physician could see the patient. "We believe Miss Sterling was drugged, Doctor. Later, someone tried to smother her. The pillow he held over her face is there on the floor, and you will see there are bruises forming beneath the lady's eyes and along the curve of her jaw."

With the efficiency of his calling, the doctor shooed everyone from the room, all save Lady Worthing, so he could examine the patient. When he was finished, he confirmed what Matthew had said and prescribed a day of bed rest for Sarah. "She may have some broth and toast for supper," he instructed her ladyship, "then if she feels more the thing tomorrow, she may have a nice piece of fowl."

Sarah tried to convince the kind, elderly gentleman that she did not need to remain in bed all day, but the effort was just too exhausting for her. She laid her head back and closed her eyes for a moment to recoup her strength, and the next time she woke, the afternoon sun was shining though her bedchamber window, its rays revealing the shower of dust motes floating through the air.

The door to her bedchamber was open, and Matthew Donaldson stood just outside the room. "Did you find anything missing?" he asked.

"No, sir," Morag answered. "Her things were a proper mess, they were, like someone had been searching for sommit, but I can't find nothing missing. Unless," she said, then paused.

"Unless," Matthew prompted.

"Unless it were in the dressing table. Miss keeps her private things in those drawers, and I don't never touch them."

Morag's words sent a feeling of foreboding through Sarah's entire body, and while Matthew questioned the young maid about her own health, inquiring if the servant felt any ill effects from the drugged tea she had drunk, Sarah slipped from beneath the covers and more or less stumbled across the room to the dressing table. As she stood in that spot where the shadowed intruder had stood, she ignored the gooseflesh that crept up her arms, concentrating instead upon the small prayer she sent to heaven—a prayer that she would find her father's book where she had left it the night before.

Slowly she pulled the delicate handle, urging the drawer open. When she looked inside, tears pooled in her eyes and spilled down her cheeks, for the drawer was empty. The loaded pistol and the leather-bound book of formulas were gone.

"I came," Chloe said, "to bid you good-bye, and to tell you how much I enjoyed making your acquaintance."

"Good-bye?" Sarah repeated, turning from the gallery window where she had watched the last of the twilight give way to the sparkle of a thousand stars. "I do not understand. Are you leaving?"

The girl nodded, making her dusky curls bounce. "Aunt Agatha has called for the carriage to be ready quite early tomorrow morning. We are bound for Worth Park, in Sussex." The pink of rose petals colored her cheeks, making her eyes look bluer than a summer sky. "Noel is to accompany us to my home. He wishes to speak with my father."

Knowing what this meant, Sarah smiled. And

though it was the first smile she had managed since discovering the loss of her father's book that afternoon, it was no less genuine for the tears that still glistened on her lashes. "I am very happy for you both. Mr. Kemp is everything that is most admirable in a gentleman, and I am persuaded he will make you a kind and considerate husband."

An even deeper blush was the young lady's only reply to that observation.

Impulsively, Chloe crossed the space that divided them and caught Sarah's hands, squeezing them. "My one regret," she said, "is that we leave at this time, when so much unpleasantness has occurred. I feel almost as though we are abandoning you and Mr. Donaldson when you have most need of your friends."

"You must not think that, for I do not. And I cannot believe that Mr. Donaldson would either. Actually, the investigation may go much smoother without so many people in the house. I have no personal knowledge of Bow Street runners, but I should imagine the man will wish to search the entire house, and such an extensive examination will be less awkward if fewer of the rooms are occupied."

"Perhaps you are right. Still . . ."

"Think no more about it," Sarah advised, "but make me a promise to write and tell me your future plans once they are confirmed."

Chloe's smile was beautiful. "That I will most assuredly do, my dear, dear friend."

After giving Sarah a hug, the young lady turned and walked to the gallery door. She had already stepped across the threshold when she stopped and turned back. "I am so sorry about the loss of your father's color formulas, and I hope you have no regrets about telling me of the book. You cannot know how flattered I was that you confided something important to me;

especially when I discovered that you had shared the information with no one else."

At the mention of her father's book, moisture filled Sarah's eyes. She thought she had shed enough tears for a lifetime, but apparently the supply was endless. Garrick Sterling had kept those formulas a secret, guarding them like the treasures they were, trusting them to no one but his daughter, and Sarah could not quell the guilt she felt at losing her father's life's work.

In telling Chloe Worthing, Sarah had betrayed her father's trust, and she had regretted that one foolish lapse more than she could say. Of course, it would be unpardonably churlish now to tell the young lady that she had wished the words back the moment they had crossed her lips. The time had passed for such repining, so she cleared her throat and willed the tears away.

"How could I regret telling you," she said, "when you vowed that you would honor my secret."

The young lady appeared inordinately interested in a simple gold ring she wore on her little finger, turning the circle back and forth several times. "And I did honor it," she said quietly, "honestly I did. Except for that one slip."

Every nerve in Sarah's body rushed to the surface, and her skin actually hurt with the waiting to hear what Chloe meant. "Slip?" she said. "I do not understand. Are you saying that you told someone about my father's book?"

"I did," she said, "and I do most humbly beg your pardon. However. I am persuaded the man is trustworthy, for I understand he has been the steward at Donmore Hall for nearly a quarter of a century. Newsome, I believe he is called."

After Chloe left, Sarah waited only until her hands were steady enough to turn the key in the gallery door, then she hurried down the corridor to the back stairs, deciding upon that route as the quickest way to the steward's office at the rear of the house. Chloe had told Angus Newsome about the book, and now the book was gone. If he was the person who took it, Sarah would know soon enough, for she meant to confront him. If he so much as flinched, she would force him to confess.

Using the corridor door she had passed through the first day she came to Donmore Hall, Sarah entered the steward's domain. It looked much as she remembered it. A battered desk made of deal pine dominated the small room, and a cabinet of some sort stood flush with the inner wall. The office was empty save for those two pieces and a ladder-back chair, and though a number of papers lay upon the blotter that covered the surface of the desk, the room had an unoccupied feeling about it, as though no one had been in or out the entire day.

Spurred by her desire to find the book, Sarah tossed aside any scruples she may have had about rifling through another person's property and went directly to the desk. Taking the pewter candlestick that stood on the mantel above the fireplace, she lit the single work candle and set it on the edge of the blotter. Then she pulled out the shallow drawer above the kneehole and began to search through its contents. The little leather-bound book was not there.

A similar investigation of the three drawers to the right revealed nothing. Likewise, the topmost drawer to the left contained nothing but copies of letters Angus Newsome had written over the years in his capacity as steward to Mr. Carlton Donaldson. It was when Sarah pulled open the bottom drawer, which was constructed to look like two, that she knew for certain the steward had been the shadow figure in her room last night—the man who had come very near to murdering her.

Lying atop a large, battered ledger and an empty metal cash drawer was a short pocket pistol, the same double-barrel weapon Garrick Sterling had insisted his daughter carry with her for protection.

It was while she examined the pistol, to be absolutely certain it was her papa's, that Sarah heard someone coming down the corridor. Hoping it might be Newsome, she blew out the flame of the candle and ducked down beneath the kneehole of the desk. With a weapon in her hand, she felt certain she could make the steward tell her what he had done with the book.

While she hid, someone opened the door and looked inside. Sarah held her breath. It was a man; she could tell that much from the heavy thud of his boots on the bare floor.

He stepped inside the room, pausing just on the other side of the desk, and for several seconds he did not move. He seemed to be listening for something, and when he sniffed the air, then reached across the blotter and tested the candle wick with his thumb and finger, Sarah decided it was time to reveal her presence.

"Stay just where you are," she said, scrambling to her feet. "I have a pistol, and I am not afraid to use it."

"So, madam," Matthew Donaldson said, "after all this time, you have finally decided to shoot me."

"Matthew! I thought you were Angus Newsome."

"I am relieved to hear it."

He reached across the desk and relit the candle, then moving carefully, he placed his fingers over hers until the pistol was pointed downward. "Now," he said, easing the weapon from her hand and setting it on the blotter, "suppose you tell me why you feel justified in threatening my steward."

"It was he who attacked me and stole my father's book."

Matthew's face appeared calm, but his gray eyes were dark as a storm-tossed sea. "Not that I doubt your word, but have you proof? Accusing a man of attempted murder is a serious thing."

She pointed to the pistol, just in case he had not given it sufficient attention. "I found that in his desk. It is Papa's."

"Can you be certain? Is it initialed? Or is it marked in any way that would distinguish it from possibly hundreds of other pistols made by that particular gunsmith?"

"No, but—"

"Did you find your father's book?" he asked quietly.

"No."

"Or did you, perchance, discover some evidence that would prove it was Angus Newsome who took the paintings from the gallery? A letter? A bill of sale?"

She shook her head. "But I have not searched that cabinet."

Without another word, Matthew stepped over to the cabinet, opened the doors, and began searching through the books and boxes on the three shelves. "There is nothing here," he said after the final shelf had been examined.

Terribly disappointed at the news, Sarah sat down in the ladder-black chair. Her throat was tight, and it took all her resolve to suppress the tears that had flowed all afternoon like water from a fountain. "I was so certain."

"What made you think it might be Newsome?"

"Chloe told him about the book of color formulas."

"And is that your only cause for suspecting the man? That he knew of the book's existence?"

It seemed to Sarah that Matthew was defending the steward. "Is that not enough?"

He shook his head. "I think not, for if knowing about the book is your sole basis for assigning guilt, who is to say the thief was not Chloe? The same reasoning principle would apply."

"It was certainly not Chloe Worthing who tried to smother me! Furthermore, when I first met her, she did not have cuts and bruises all over her face. The same cannot be said for Newsome. It occurred to me, while I was searching his desk, that perhaps the steward might have run afoul of that Cockney fellow even before that day in the mist."

"Again," Matthew said, "the presence of bruises proves nothing. After all," he continued, the words surprisingly soft, "there are smudges on your lovely face."

For some reason, his saying hers was a lovely face broke Sarah's resolve, and she put her elbows on the desk top and hid her face in her hands. No sound escaped her lips, but tears spilled through her fingers, tears she was unable to stop.

It was inconceivable that a mere twenty-four hours could wreak such havoc upon her emotions. Fear clung to her much as her damp dress had done the night she was caught in the rain, for she could not forget the pressure of the pillow upon her face. As well, guilt gnawed at her insides for having told anyone about her father's book. In her entire life she had never felt so defenseless or so lonely.

"Sarah," Matthew said, his voice hesitant, low. "Do not cry. Please. I cannot bear to see you suffer, to know that you are in pain. We will find the book, I make you that promise."

At that moment, when she felt so alone, the book—everything—was of only secondary importance. All Sarah could think of was how much she needed to be comforted, how much she needed to be close to Matthew. More than close. She wanted his arms

around her. She yearned to feel his strength; to be sur-
rounded by it. And the yearning made her tremble.

Calling herself a fool for wanting what she could not
have, she raised her head and used the sleeve of her
dress to wipe away the tears that had wet her cheeks.
Through still-damp lashes she stared across the space
that divided her from Matthew. He stood beside the
cabinet, looking tall and reassuringly powerful, and
when their gazes met, his eyes were filled with compassion, and something else she dared not name. The
air between them seemed to thicken, and Sarah was
obliged to breathe very deeply to force the needed
oxygen into her lungs.

"Newsome lives in the gatehouse," Matthew said. "I
will go down there this instant and search the place
from top to bottom. If the book is there, I will bring it
back to you."

"No," she said, fighting the emotion that nearly
choked her. "Do not go. Not now."

Where she found the nerve to make the first move,
she did not know, but unable to ignore the force that
urged her on, she rose from the chair, stepped around
the desk, and walked directly to him, stopping so close
that mere inches separated them.

"Matthew," she whispered, "I . . ." Not knowing
how to tell him what she needed, she followed some
primal instinct and leaned forward, laying her cheek
against his chest.

For several moments he stood still as a tree, then he
muttered something beneath his breath and his arms
stole around her, gathering her close.

He held her gently, as though she might break, his
cheek resting against the top of her head. Sarah
thought she felt his lips upon her hair, and very slowly
she lifted her face toward his, an inch at a time, being
careful not to lose contact with his chest.

Now his lips were touching her forehead. They were

warm upon her skin. She paused for just a moment, her heart beating so hard it threatened to burst right out of her chest, then she eased onto her tiptoes until the corner of her mouth replaced her forehead beneath his lips.

She waited, not wanting to push herself upon him if he was unwilling, then almost imperceptibly his lips moved against the corner of her mouth. Weak with relief, she turned that extra inch, offering him her entire mouth, to do with as he wished.

Thankfully, he seemed to wish to do exactly what she wished to have done, and when he covered her mouth with his own, Sarah wound her arms around his waist and pressed against him, delighting in his strength and closeness.

At first the kiss was warm and gentle, the sweetness of discovery enough, but as the kiss continued, something changed and the sweetness slowly blossomed into a flame—a heat that scorched Sarah to her very soul. And like a moth, she longed to throw herself into that flame.

Knowing this was madness, Matthew reached behind his back and loosened her arms, then he slowly eased her away from him. "Sarah," he said, his breath coming in quick gulps, as if he had been running. "Sweet, beautiful Sarah."

"Matthew," she murmured.

At the sound of his name upon her kiss-softened lips, his heart and his mind—his entire being—implored him to take her back into his arms.

She tried to draw close to him again, but he caught her shoulders and held her away. "Do not," he said.

"But . . . but why? I thought you would like to kiss me. When I first arrived at the Hall, you said—"

"Never mind what I said!"

Confusion and hurt darkened her eyes, and the sight of them was like a blow to Matthew's heart.

"Is it something I did?" she asked. "Perhaps I did not do it right. Is that it?"

"No. Of course not."

The pink of embarrassment crept into her cheeks. "Is it because I came to you, instead of waiting for you to come to me?"

Damnation! He felt as though he had just kicked a newborn kitten. But how could he tell an innocent like Sarah about the type of women he had known? How could he explain to her the kind of life he had led? He could not, for no matter what he said, the truth of the matter was that he was not worthy of her.

"You do not understand," he said.

"Then explain it to me so that I can understand. What did I do wrong?"

"You did nothing wrong. In fact, you did everything wonderfully right. It is just that you deserve more—much more than I am capable of giving."

The pink in her cheeks became bright red, and when she lowered her head as if to hide the fact, Matthew put his finger beneath her chin and urged her to look at him once again.

"Forgive me," he said, "for this is all my fault. You were vulnerable, and I knew it. I should have been more guarded. Especially when I knew nothing could ever come of our friendship."

Nothing could ever come of our friendship. Sarah could not believe the pain those words inflicted, even though he was merely being truthful. Of course nothing could come of their friendship; she had known that all along. Matthew Donaldson was a wealthy man—a gentleman who would be welcome in the most exalted society—and she was his employee, the person hired to clean and restore his art collection.

When she stepped back, he let go of her shoulders, and without his support, she felt even lonelier than before.

He had said this was all his fault, but they both knew better. Sarah had come to him, all but obliging him to hold her in his arms and kiss her. Taking the blame upon himself was but a gentleman's way of softening the truth—the simple truth that she was not gentlewoman enough for him to marry.

"I am sorry," she said. The words caught in her throat, making her sound as though she might start crying again. But she would not do that! Even if suppressing the tears ultimately choked her, she would not give vent to them in front of Matthew Donaldson.

After gathering up what little pride she had left, Sarah returned to the desk and retrieved the pistol. "I am not wrong about Angus Newsome," she said. "Nor am I wrong about the ownership of this weapon. I believe it is the same one I brought with me to Northumberland, just as surely as I believe that your steward is the person who stole your artwork and my father's book.

"And," she added, "I intend to prove it."

Chapter Thirteen

Sarah walked away from the steward's office, and Matthew, with as much dignity as she could summon; then, with the pistol hidden in the folds of her skirt, she went to the vestibule in search of a footman. "Will you please find Morag," she asked the man, "and inform her that I will be in the gallery. Tell her that she is not to wait up for me."

"Yes, miss."

While the servant went to do her bidding, Sarah lit one of the candles left on the console table each evening for the convenience of the guests, and climbed the front stairs. The thought of spending another night in the yellow bedchamber, after what had happened there, was more than she could contemplate, so she went directly to the gallery, the one place where she could be assured of both security and privacy.

As always, she found it calming to be among the lovely paintings. Also, since she had been given charge of the key to the door, she was able to lock herself in the room without worrying about another confrontation with Angus Newsome, the man she believed had tried to smother her the night before.

She had only just set the candle and the pistol on the worktable when she heard the heavy crunch of hooves on the gravel carriageway. Was that Matthew on his way to the gatehouse? He had said he would go down to the steward's quarters to search for her father's book, but that had been before she threw herself at him, all but begging him to hold her—to love her.

After such an embarrassing debacle, she supposed a gentleman could be forgiven if the promise he made slipped his mind. Somehow, though, she did not believe he would forget. Not Matthew.

After hurrying to the window, she pressed her face against the cool pane in an attempt to see who rode away from the Hall. Unfortunately, it was too dark to discern more than the outline of horse and rider. It might have been Matthew, but it might just as easily have been one of the servants bound for the village, his objective a pint at the Red Lion.

She watched until man and horse disappeared around the stand of ancient holm oak trees; then, with no way to be certain of the identity of the rider, she turned from the window. If it was Matthew, and he found her father's book, he would waste no time in returning it to her. Even if he found nothing, he would probably wish to tell her that as well. In any event, she had no recourse but to wait.

Matthew had not been as skeptical of Sarah's theory about Angus Newsome as he had led her to believe. He had played the role of devil's advocate for no other reason than to calm Sarah's zeal. She was one of those rare and special people who see a wrong and set about immediately to right it, without weighing the costs to themselves, and he was afraid she might confront the man, putting herself in further danger.

For Matthew, it was torture standing there in the steward's office, knowing he could do nothing to allay her fears. Looking at her lovely face, with the bruises turning darker by the hour, he could well imagine what she must have gone through, and the image made his chest ache as though a giant being had reached in and plucked out his heart. If Sarah were to act upon her suspicions, and something worse befell her, Matthew feared he would never forgive himself. If she was hurt again, he might never again find relief from that ache.

In light of Sarah's information, it appeared that Angus Newsome might well be the blackguard who had attacked her. From the time Matthew took up residence at Donmore Hall, he had distrusted the steward. Despite the man's seeming loyalty to Carlton Donaldson, there was an aura of bitterness about him, and Matthew had seen enough such men in the army to know they were quick to justify any cruel or dishonest act they committed.

I didn't get my fair share. I deserved it. I never had a chance. Matthew had heard all the excuses.

Still, he had waited about making any changes at the Hall until he had been there long enough to give each employee an opportunity to prove his or her worth. Newsome had performed his job as steward competently, and though Matthew disliked him, there was no evidence of wrongdoing and no justification for dismissing him.

Sarah's arguments made good sense. Only two people other than she knew of Garrick Sterling's book, and of those two, only one would have had the strength to hold a pillow over Sarah's face until she lost consciousness. Also, Newsome was nowhere to be found that day, and though an unexplained absence was not enough to convict a man of a crime, it was enough to rouse suspicion. It was certainly enough to prompt Matthew to ride to the gatehouse for a look around.

He had promised Sarah that he would find the book, and he would not rest until that promise was fulfilled; therefore, as soon as she left the office, he went to the stable and had the gelding saddled.

The moon was at the crescent stage, but the stars

were plentiful and there was sufficient light to see
where they were going. They followed the carriageway as it meandered around the oaks, but once the
small sandstone house was in view, Matthew led the
horse off the gravel into the quieter grass. No point in
announcing their arrival. If Newsome was there, an
unexpected visit might prove less dangerous.

"Whoa, boy," he whispered, halting the chestnut
while they were still several yards from their ultimate
destination. Matthew was certain he had seen the
glow of candlelight in one of the dormer windows, but
now all was dark. Had he been spotted?

"Better to be safe than sorry," he said, alighting from
the horse and leading the animal around to the rear of
the house.

Stopping beside a lone and stunted larch, he looped
the chestnut's reins around a limb of the tree then
crept toward the front of the house, being careful to
crouch low as he passed the darkened windows. He
had only just arrived at the door when he heard a foot-
fall behind him. Instantly, something hard and unfor-
giving hit the side of his head, and as a thousand
shards of pain pierced his brain, he fell to the ground.
Matthew knew his attacker stood over him, for he felt
a hard-toed boot prod him none too gently in the ribs.
Within moments, however, unrelieved blackness de-
scended and he knew no more.

Sarah woke with a start. It was no longer night, and
she had fallen asleep at the worktable, a letter to her father only half written and the quill still in her hand.
The candle had burned down in its holder, leaving a
pool of wax on the surface of the table, and a gray light
showed at the windows. Sarah remembered that eerie,
diffused light; she had seen it for the first time a little
more than a fortnight ago.

She rose and stretched, trying to work the kinks

from her neck and shoulders, then walked over to look out. It was mist, right enough, and once again the world was cloaked in it, limiting visibility to mere inches. This time, however, she would not be so foolish as to wander about in it; she would remember Matthew's warning about the dangers of such weather.

Matthew! Had he returned only to find the gallery door locked? Perhaps he had knocked, and that was what had awakened her. He might even now have her father's book in his possession.

Hoping that was so, she hurried to the door, turned the key in the lock, then walked across the hall to knock at the door of the master bedchamber. "Matthew," she called, "it is Sarah. Did you try to wake me?"

Silence greeted her query. "Matthew," she called again, only louder. "Are you there?"

When there was still no reply, she opened the door just wide enough to see if he was asleep. The bed had not been slept in. She had no idea what time it was, but it felt early, much too early for the maids to have already straightened his room.

Uneasiness began to gnaw at her, but she told herself there could be many explanations for why he had not slept in his bed. After all, she had not slept in hers. He might have come in and gone straight to his book room to write a letter. Or there was always the possibility that he had not gone out at all.

Deciding there was but one way to know for certain if he was at home, she made her way down the stairs to the library. When she found that room empty, and the morning fire as yet unlit, her earlier uneasiness became fear. Where could Matthew be?

She was convinced now that he had been the rider she had watched gallop up the carriageway last evening, and just as convinced that he could have had only one destination. And he had not returned.

Sarah had no idea what she should do; all she knew was that she must do something. But what? Short of going to the gatehouse herself, she had no way of discovering if Matthew was still there, or if he had ever been there. It was little more than half a mile from the Hall to the end of the carriageway, and normally she could walk that distance in a matter of minutes. Unfortunately, with the mist obscuring everything for miles, it was too dangerous to venture as far as ten feet.

When Matthew had rescued her the first day she was at the Hall, she had told him that she tried never to make the same mistake twice. "Rest assured," she had said, "I will not be so foolish as to go outside in such weather a second time." And yet, she was contemplating just such a move, for how could she stay inside, comfortable and secure, while Matthew might be hurt—or worse.

She could not—would not—do so!

The decision made to find Matthew, she ran up to the yellow bedchamber to don her walking boots and the French gray mantle, then she stopped by the gallery to collect her father's pistol. Before she slipped the weapon into the pocket sewn in the lining of the cape, she said a quick prayer that she would not stumble and shoot herself in the side.

Sarah would have liked to fetch one of the footmen to go with her, but her conscience would not allow her to do so. The mists were dangerous, and she could not ask a man to risk his life for what might prove nothing more than a wild-goose chase.

"Stay on the gravel," she said aloud, the sound all but swallowed up in the mist. "As long as you can hear that crunch beneath your boots, you cannot become lost."

Not as naive as she had been the other time she had ventured out blindly in such weather, Sarah had the good sense to be frightened. However, she had not come outside without a plan. Aware that the place where the carriageway meandered around the stand of oak trees was about halfway to the gate, she had begun counting her steps the moment she was outside the front entrance. Once she rounded the trees, she would merely count backward from the last number. When she reached the final five, she should be opposite the gatehouse. At least, she hoped so.

Though not as confident as she might have been in her strategy, at least it kept her thoughts from straying to what might have happened to Matthew. Also, she was obliged to concentrate on keeping her pace as consistent as possible and on not forgetting her count.

By the time she reached the trees, she had taken six hundred and sixty steps; now, all she had to do was reverse the number and pray she had reckoned correctly.

"Ten," she said several minutes later. "Nine. Eight. Seven. Six." She stopped. "This is it."

After executing a quarter turn to her left, Sarah moved cautiously, stopping the instant her boot touched ungraveled land.

If she remembered correctly, the gatehouse was not more than fifteen feet from the edge of the carriageway. Therefore, if she had erred in her basic strategy, she would know it as soon as she had taken seven or eight steps. Able to detect vague shapes within her arm's reach, she was not afraid of bumping into the house; her fear was of missing it by a few feet and not knowing whether to adjust to her left or to her right.

After saying a prayer, she inhaled deeply then took

the first step. "One," she whispered. "Two. Three. Four. Five. Six. Seven. Ooph!"

Fooled by the paleness of the sandstone, she had bumped into the house after all. Much too grateful to complain, however, she slipped her arms through the braided vents on either side of her mantle and placed her palms flat against the sandstone, using her hands to guide her to the door. The first attempt ended at the corner of the building, but she did not despair. She merely felt her way back the way she had come, then continued in that direction.

When her hands encountered the wooden jamb, then the opening, and finally the door itself, she offered another prayer, one of thanksgiving. "And please," she whispered, "let Matthew be here."

Striving to be as quiet as possible, she lifted the latch and eased the thick wooden door open. She had moved it no more than a foot when the wood was suddenly yanked from her hands, causing her to fall into the room, where she landed face down on the hard stone floor.

"So," Angus Newsome said, his tone a mockery of the cordial host, "we've another visitor. The meddlesome Miss Sterling. Come in, come in. You are welcome. Though I must say it is a bit of a surprise seeing you, especially looking so well."

While she struggled to get up off the cold floor, the steward lit a candle and brought it close, holding it in his left hand. Even in the dim light, Sarah could see most of the small, sparsely furnished room, though her attention was caught fast by the item in the man's right hand. It was a pistol, the kind men carried in holsters on their saddles, and the long barrel and metal-covered grip end made it appear ominous.

"Close the door," he ordered.

Sarah obeyed. She had no other choice, for she had spied a pair of gentleman's black leather riding boots beside the empty fireplace. They belonged to Matthew, she was certain of it, and she would not leave this house without him.

When the door was shut, Newsome commended her obedience, his tone sarcastic. "Keeps out the drafts. And we wouldn't want Mr. Donaldson to take a chill, now would we? I regret to say he has already met with a nasty accident."

At Sarah's gasp, the steward laughed. "Oh, do not repine overmuch, Miss Sterling, for our employer is not dead, merely injured. Though I should warn you, his future health depends entirely upon you and your continued cooperation."

"Where is he?"

Newsome held the candle high and to his right so that it cast a bit more light into the far corner of the room. There, sitting in a ladder-back chair, with his hands bound cruelly behind him, was Matthew. A cloth of some kind had been stuffed inside his mouth, then his own handkerchief had been used to hold the first cloth in place.

Seeing him like that sent a sick shudder through Sarah. However, the thing she found even more frightening than his being bound and gagged, was the dark stain that began at his hairline and ran down his left temple and cheek.

"You blackguard! What have you done to him?"

"My, my. Such passion." Newsome showed her the metal-covered grip of his pistol. "I merely gave him a tap on the noggin with this. He is not dead, as you may see for yourself."

Not waiting for a second invitation, Sarah hurried to the corner and knelt down beside Matthew. This close, she could see that his eyes were open, though they registered no joy at seeing her.

Without asking permission of their captor, she worked the handkerchief down past Matthew's chin and removed the cloth from his mouth. Then, very gently, she pushed aside the lock of dark hair that covered the wound at the side of his head. The blood that had run down his face was dry, and the gash in his skin had ceased to bleed. "Are you in pain?" she asked.

He was obliged to swallow several times before he could speak, and when he finally managed a few words, his concern was not for himself but for her. "Why did you come?" he asked, his voice filled with regret.

"When you did not return, I had to find you. I was so worried about you."

"This is all very touching," Newsome said, setting the candlestick back on the mantelpiece, "but I should be pleased, Miss Sterling, if you would take a seat on the floor there by the, er, gentleman. Not being in the habit of entertaining visitors, so to speak, I was caught unawares and have no more rope. So you will humor me by remaining very still."

"I can do that," she said. "I can be still as a mouse."

"A wise decision, for should you decide to move, be warned, I will shoot you."

"I believe you," she said. Still on her knees, she moved to Matthew's left, staying so close to him her shoulder pressed against his hip, then she sat back on her heels. After arranging the hem of her mantle very primly around her lap, she pulled her arms back through the braided vents out of sight. "Why should I not believe you?" she continued. "After all, you did nearly smother me."

"An unplanned and poorly executed move," he said. "Though if you had drunk all the nice tea I left at your bedchamber door, I would not have needed to resort to violence."

Sarah could not believe his self-justification. "Are you saying it was my fault?"

"There was no one in the room but you and me, so it must have been you."

"But why?" she asked. "What did I ever do to you?"

"You got in my way. I needed that book of formulas as a bargaining tool. I would have taken another painting instead, but your being at the Hall made it difficult for me to visit the gallery long enough to choose wisely. The last time, I just took what was closest to hand, but it turned out to be only a copy. When the man who paid me for it discovered it was not an original, he was very angry."

"Was it he who beat you?"

"Sarah," Matthew cautioned, "do not say anything more."

"Oh, I don't mind answering her questions. Until the mist burns away, I got no place to go. I might as well talk as not. Just let me get comfortable."

While Newsome's attention was centered on dragging another ladder-back chair away from the wall, Sarah slipped her right arm through the vent in her mantle, keeping very erect so her movements could not be seen. Gently she placed her hand on Matthew's bound wrists, then she felt all around the knots in the rope to see if she could possibly untie them. At her touch, he grew very still, but otherwise he remained as before, his cool gray stare focused on Newsome, taking care not to give Sarah away.

"All females being as curious as cats," the steward said, settling into the chair, "I suppose you're wondering how I came to take the first painting?"

"I am," she replied, hoping the sarcasm was not detectable in her voice. "Was it something old Mr. Donaldson did? Did he bring it upon himself?"

He blinked in surprise. "Say, you're right smart for a female. It was *all* his fault. He abused my trust. Made promises he didn't keep. If he had treated me fair, I never would have taken anything."

Matthew sat straight as a post, taking no part in the conversation, while Sarah worked at loosening the first knot. "Are you trying to tell us," she said, "that Carlton Donaldson went back on employment promises made to you?"

"That's exactly what he did. I came to Donmore Hall more than twenty years ago. At that time, the old man was in his sixtieth year, and he no longer cared for the running of the estate. The art collection was all that interested him."

"It did not interest you?" she asked.

He shook his head. "I knew aught of such things. I was a young man then, only seven-and-twenty, and I had been steward at a much smaller estate owned by a widow in Surrey."

Anger shone in his dull green eyes. "I thought this was my opportunity to make something of myself, for the old man said if I would come to Northumberland, he would see I was remembered in his will."

"His will? Ooh, how nice."

Sarah already knew about Carlton Donaldson's will, having overheard the two gossips at the Fairlies' dinner party, but she wanted to keep the steward talking. The knot was definitely getting looser.

"Five thousand, that old martinet promised me, so I came north, and I stayed in this cold, rugged, lonely land, where the winters last forever and the people are suspicious of anyone whose father and grandfather were not born in the north country. And all that time I dulled my loneliness by remembering the five thousand pounds and the little cottage I would buy not too far from London."

Matthew very wisely let her do what she could to the rope, without trying to help, but she could feel the tension in his body.

"What happened?" she asked when Newsome had remained quiet for too long.

"The old man got older. As he neared eighty, he began to forget things: my name, what year it was, things like that. One day, just to remind him, I asked would he advance me a hundred from my five thousand so I could take a holiday. I hadn't left the place for more than a twelve-month, and though I had enough put by for a short stay, a hundred would not have come amiss."

"A reasonable enough request," she said.

"You'd think so," he agreed. "But the old man came the ugly. 'What five thousand?' he says. 'You get your salary same as the other servants. Who said you deserved more?' Then he accused me of doctoring the books to pad my own pockets."

Sarah tsk-tsked, and the steward leaned forward, caught up in his own story.

"Of course, the next day the old fool had forgotten the incident, so I told myself he really had put me in his will, it had just slipped his mind."

Sarah's fingernails broke one after another as she worked at the rope, but she felt certain she needed just a few minutes more to loosen the knots. "What happened then?"

"Then, after an illness that kept him in bed for the better part of the winter, the old stiff rump began accusing the staff of stealing things. Had his valet carry him into the gallery, and once there, he counted the paintings, insisting that one was missing. There weren't any missing as I could see, but he said one was gone.

"When I brought him the inventory and showed him that the count still matched, he accused me of changing the number. Threatened to turn me out on the spot, without a reference. He even said he was writing a letter to Bow Street in London, to send up a runner. Said he'd see me in Newgate Prison."

Sarah gasped dramatically. "Newgate! That is a ter-

rible place. I live in London, so I know. But I interrupted you. Please, do go on."

"Well," he continued, a smug look upon his face,
"about that time, Mr. Noel Kemp showed up with a
brand-new carriage and a bang-up pair of horses. I
never liked Kemp, so when the old man wanted to
know where his heir got the money for the purchase, I
suggested maybe the young man had been the one to
take the painting, to support his way of life."

He laughed at the memory. "Old stiff rump went
into a rage and threw Kemp out that very day, then he
sent for his solicitor, said he was changing his will."

He laughed again, smug in his recollection. "That
was when I got the idea. What was to keep me from
taking a few of the smaller paintings and selling them?
After all, I had earned that five thousand, and if I
didn't take it before the old man put his spoon in the
wall, chances were I would never see it. So I took two
paintings from the gallery and put two I found in the
attic in their places so if he counted them again, the
tally would be the same as before."

"Ingenious," Sarah said.

"I thought so. Later, when I knew the new owner
was coming, I burned the inventory so he wouldn't
know the correct count, then I took the two replace-
ments back up to the attic and helped myself to a third
picture from the gallery, a pretty lady in a white dress.
Only that painting turned out to be a fake."

He scowled at Sarah as though the copy had been
her fault.

"I had written to Mr. Wayford that I was bringing
the portrait when I came to London, so he lined up a
buyer. When the painting turned out to be a fake,
Wayford had his lads beat me up, said I had made him
lose face. That's when he started threatening me, said
if I didn't bring him a proper work, he would see I disappeared for good."

The knot had finally come loose, enough so Matthew could free his wrists, and while he flexed his fingers to get the circulation going, Sarah slipped her arm back beneath her cape and removed her papa's pistol from the inside pocket.

Being careful not to move too quickly and give herself away, she eased the short-barreled pistol into Matthew's hands.

Chapter Fourteen

Matthew felt the cold metal touch his fingers and knew instantly what Sarah had done. Clever, clever girl! He still could not believe she had braved the mist to search for him, and now here she was pressing a weapon into his hands. A weapon that would even the confrontation between Angus Newsome and himself, an encounter he looked forward to with anticipation.

"Speaking of Newgate Prison," Matthew said, still not moving, "I think you had better plan for a visit there after all."

"Oh, I had, had I? First, I would have to be caught."

Matthew's tone was quiet, conversational. "I think that can be arranged."

Newsome scoffed. "Ha! And who'll be doing the catching? You?"

"That possibility should not be overlooked."

"You're as daft as that old martinet who preceded you if you think—"

"What I think," Matthew said, standing suddenly and aiming the small double-barrel pistol at the steward's head, "is that you should lay down your weapon and put up your hands."

If Matthew had suddenly sprouted wings, Angus Newsome would not have been more surprised, and in his haste to stand, he tumbled out of his own chair. Righting himself, he pointed his pistol at Matthew.

"How the deuce did you get free? And who gave you that barker?"

Ignoring the question, Matthew said, "Did you think I would just sit here and let you steal from me, and from Miss Sterling, and do nothing about it?" He turned sideways and raised his arm shoulder height, bringing the pistol that much closer to Newsome's heart. "Now do as I say, and put down your weapon."

Newsome stared at Sarah, who had risen to her feet. "It was you, wasn't it? This is all your fault. I should have shot you the moment you fell into the room."

His face began to twitch, and his voice sounded as though he were trying not to cry. "You'll pay for this!" he said, then he suddenly took aim at Sarah.

"No!" Matthew yelled. Not waiting to see what might happen, he pulled the trigger of the little pocket pistol, firing one bullet. It hit Newsome between the second and third buttons of his waistcoat.

"What the—" Surprise widened the man's eyes, and he looked down at his chest as though he could not believe this was happening to him. As the blood began to spill from the wound, he looked up at Matthew and fired.

Matthew gasped as a blaze straight from hell seemed to burst into flame inside his shoulder, and while he took aim to discharge the second bullet at Newsome, the man slumped forward and fell to the floor.

Sarah had watched a man prepare to kill her, and she had ceased to breathe. Now that the awful exchange of gunfire was finished, she had to tell herself to fill her lungs, giving herself instruction as though it were a heretofore untried activity. *In. Out. In. Out.*

She had not been frightened, there had been no time for such a luxury, but now as she looked at the man who lay on the floor, his life's blood deserting him in rapid pumping motion, she began to tremble. But for

Matthew's quickness, the person on the floor would have been her.

"Matthew, I—"

The words froze in her throat when she turned to the man who had saved her life—the man she loved—for blood gushed from him as quickly as it flowed from Angus Newsome.

"You are hurt!"

"Only a little." Even as he said the words, he swayed, and Sarah was obliged to grab his arm and help him sit down again before he fell.

After untying the handkerchief that was still around his neck, she folded the linen and pressed it against the wound in his shoulder. Within less time than it took to fold, the cloth was red with blood. "You need help," she said. "More than I know how to give."

"Can you get my horse?" he asked. "I left him tied to a tree behind the gatehouse. If he is still there, and you could bring him around to the door, I could ride him to the Hall. My valet was at Salamanca, and he knows about tending wounds. He will have me fixed up in no time."

Sarah took leave to doubt that last statement, but she kept her opinion to herself; especially since denying how badly Matthew was hurt was all that kept her from surrendering to a much deserved fit of the vapors.

"I will get the chestnut," she said.

It was a draw as to which she wanted less to do: go back out into the mist, or catch a spirited steed that had been left out all night. Because both those activities were preferable to leaving Matthew to die, Sarah stepped around Newsome's lifeless body, opened the door, and went outside to fetch the gelding.

Running her hand along the sandstone outer wall of the house, she found the front right corner, then she continued around until she found the rear corner.

"Horse," she called into the mist, "are you there, horse?"

To her surprise, she heard a whicker only a little way to her left. "Good boy," she said, then she held her arms straight out in front of her to shield herself in case she bumped into the animal and made it more frightened than it probably already was.

Counting aloud, she took the first few steps. "One. Two. Three."

Before she could give voice to the next number, her right hand touched wet horseflesh. The skin twitched beneath her palm, making Sarah flinch, but when the horse did not kick out at her or turn to bite her, she patted the strong flank and felt her way up past the mane to the forelock.

"Good horse," she said, catching hold of his head-gear. "Let me find your reins, there's a good boy, and I will take you to your master."

Untying his reins was easy, even without being able to see, but turning the horse without losing her way was not nearly so simple. Thankfully, she made it back to the front door without mishap. Afraid she might lose the animal if she tried to secure him someplace, she opened the door and took him inside with her.

His metal shoes clinked on the stone floor, and he tossed his head nervously as Sarah led him around Newsome's body. But when he saw Matthew, he whickered with pleasure.

"I found him," Sarah said.

Matthew's face was wan, but he managed a smile. "So I see. Do you think you can hold him a little longer, just until I can climb into the saddle? He might be a bit skittish, unaccustomed as he is to being ridden in a front parlor."

Sarah had withstood the shooting; she had even managed to pretend that the man she had stepped around was not dead. But she was not brave enough to hear Matthew jest while blood oozed from his body. Her chin began to quiver. "Matthew Donaldson! This is not funny!"

"I know, my love, and I apologize."

His love? Sarah could not believe how that endearment lifted her spirits. He did not mean it, of course, but the words sounded wonderful just the same.

Without further conversation, she caught the gelding's headgear on either side and held him steady while Matthew climbed up into the saddle. The exertion of staying upright caused beads of perspiration to form on his forehead.

"I am afraid you will have to lead him, Sarah. I am feeling rather weak, and if he gallops, I am certain to fall off."

Too much had happened for her to cavil at this latest request, so she held the chestnut's throatlatch and led him out of the gatehouse.

"Damnation!" Matthew said when he crossed the threshold and saw the gray-engulfed world. "You came out in *this*?"

"Hush," she said. "You may berate me later. For now, I must begin my counting."

By afternoon the mist was nothing but a memory. Matthew's valet had done what he could to stabilize the wound, but as soon as someone could ride to the village the doctor was summoned to remove the bullet. After the painful but productive probing, the wound was cleaned and stitched and the patient was told he was a lucky man.

"Remain in your bed for at least a week," the physician instructed. "After that time, you should be as good as new."

Upon hearing that pronouncement, Sarah returned to the yellow bedchamber, where she agreed to a hot bath and a nap upon her bed. She slept for just under twenty hours.

"You're awake," Morag said. "At last."

Sarah stretched long and slowly, wondering why she felt so stiff, then she sat up and looked around her. The window hangings were drawn, but she could see bright sunlight around the edges. "I feel marvelously refreshed. Did I nap for very long?"

Morag put her hand over her mouth to hide her smile. "Yesterday afternoon, last night, and all of this morning, miss."

"What!"

"You had me that worrit, sleeping so soundly. Though after everything you've been through, it's no wonder you were tired."

The maid walked over to the windows and opened the pretty yellow hangings, letting in the glorious afternoon sun, then she stopped at the washstand and dampened a cloth, bringing it back to Sarah. "Everyone has been coming by to see if you were awake yet, but I sent them all away."

"That was considerate of you. Thank you."

She giggled. "I'm sure you're welcome, miss, but Mr. Donaldson gave me my instructions. Said if anyone disturbed your sleep, he'd see them drawn and quartered, and me boiled in oil for letting them in the room." She laughed again. "You know the master and his funning ways."

Sarah had just pressed the wet cloth to her face, but at the mention of Matthew, she removed it so she could look at the smiling servant. "I distinctly remember the doctor recommending a week's bed rest for Mr. Donaldson. Are you telling me he is up already?"

"He come by to look in on you twice yesterday, then again this morning. But I guess he'd had enough of being an invalid, on account of when Lady Worthing,

Miss Chloe, and Mr. Kemp left a little while ago, the master got dressed and went down to see them off."

Remembering all the blood that had covered both him and the horse, and how dangerously weak Matthew had looked when the footmen carried him up to his room, Sarah muttered a word that caused the young maid's mouth to fall open. "Men!" she added. "Why must they be so obstinate? He should have done as the doctor ordered and stayed in bed."

"Her ladyship said the same, miss. Even declared herself willing to remain at the Hall a bit longer, if she was needed."

"That was good of her."

"Yes, but then her ladyship said sommit strange, miss. Sommit about you needing a chaperon."

"A chaperon! For me?"

Morag nodded. "Her ladyship seemed to think it was important, but Mr. Donaldson told her b'aint no chaperon needed on account . . ."

When the servant hesitated, Sarah urged her to finish. "Go on, please."

"Yes, miss. Mr. Donaldson said the chaperon b'aint needed on account of you wouldn't be here but another few days."

Sarah walked about the gallery, trying to draw what comfort she could from the paintings. She had felt so good when she awoke, but now, scarce an hour later, she felt listless, depressed. She supposed it was only natural for a person to feel blue-deviled after seeing one man injured and another killed; however, if she were honest, she would admit that her melancholy began the moment she heard that she was to be sent away from Donmore Hall within a few days.

How could she leave the Hall? Or more accurately, how could she leave Matthew?

Yesterday morning at the gatehouse, when she had

heard the report of Angus Newsome's pistol, then turned to discover that Matthew had been shot, his blood escaping at an alarming rate, Sarah had felt the pain as though some lethal implement had ripped through her own body.

At that moment she had known, without qualm or qualifications, that she loved Matthew Donaldson with a passion that would last forever. He had become a part of her—part of her heart, and part of her soul— and she would never love another. He might marry some acceptable girl, he might send Sarah away the very next day, but nothing would ever change the fact that she loved him completely, irrevocably, now and for eternity.

"Nothing's forever, old fellow," someone said from the carriageway below, his blustery voice carrying up to the gallery without difficulty. "Why, I graveled my place less than a year ago, and it's to be done again. Blasted nuisance, but what's the use of arguing—pays no toll, don't you know."

Sarah thought she recognized the voice as belonging to Sir Harold Fairlie, though what he should be doing here, commenting upon the Donmore carriageway, she could not even guess.

The mystery was solved in less than five minutes when Bailey scratched at the gallery door. "Begging your pardon, miss, but Sir Harold is in the book room. He would like to ask you a few questions, if you feel up to it."

"What sort of questions?"

"About Newsome, miss. Sir Harold is magistrate for Bellingham."

"Oh, yes, of course. I suppose I should have expected there to be questions."

"Shall I say you will join him directly, miss?"

"No. I will come now. To delay the inevitable is to prolong its life, and ultimately its discomfort."

"As you say, miss."

It needed only a minute or two for Sarah to reach the book room, and when she knocked at the door, it was Matthew who bid her come in.

"Sarah!" he said, leaving his place behind the desk and coming forward. His left arm rested in a sling fashioned from two white silk scarves tied together, but he held out his right hand and she caught it with both hers.

Neither of them said anything; they just stood there, holding hands and looking at one another. Sarah feasted her eyes on him, unprepared for the sheer pleasure it afforded her merely to gaze upon his face. He was as tall and handsome as ever, and if it were not for the sling, one might suppose he had never set foot inside the gatehouse.

"You are rested, madam?"

"I am rested, sir. And you? How do you feel?"

"I am well, madam. Now that I have seen you."

Sir Harold took leave to doubt the medical report. "The fellow insists he's in fine fettle, Miss Sterling, but I've two lads of my own, and I say it takes a while to mend from something as serious as a bullet wound."

Reluctantly, Sarah turned her attention away from Matthew. "Sir Harold," she said, "how do you do?"

The baronet made her as graceful a bow as his rotund middle would allow. "Your servant, ma'am. I understand you were quite the heroine yesterday."

Warmth rushed to her face. "Oh, no, sir. Nothing of the sort, I assure you."

"Well now," he said jovially, "I've no wish to dispute a lady's word, but Donaldson tells a different story."

When she said nothing more, Sir Harold let it pass. "Oh, well. I've a daughter of my own, so I know better than to push for confidences from those of your sex. However, I am required, in my official capacity, to ask you a few questions about what happened at the gate-house. That is, if you feel up to it."

When she nodded, he motioned for her to make herself comfortable in one of the red leather wing chairs. "These questions must be asked, but I will make them as brief as possible."

"Thank you, Sir Harold."

"Donaldson," he said, "you may send in Mr. Temple, if you please."

As though by prearrangement, Matthew left the room, and within seconds a large bear of a man wearing a red waistcoat beneath his bottle green coat came in and shut the door behind him. "Miss Sterling," he said, as though they had already been introduced, "I have something I believe belongs to you."

He reached inside his coat and withdrew her father's book of formulas and handed it to her.

Sarah took the little leather-bound volume and hugged it to her chest, "Oh, thank you, Mr. Temple. Thank you."

"My pleasure, ma'am."

Sir Harold motioned the man toward the desk. "Temple, there, is with Bow Street, Miss Sterling, and after I have ascertained all I need to know, he may have a question or two of his own for you."

"Ask what you will, both of you."

The interrogation was straightforward and nonconfrontational, with both men behaving as gentlemanly as possible under the circumstance. They asked for Sarah's version of what had happened, and she told it with the same orderliness and attention to detail that characterized her work. Within half an hour, Sir Harold declared himself satisfied that Newsome's death was self-defense, and the Bow Street runner concurred.

"There will be a formal inquest in a few days," Sir

Harold said. "I trust you have no plans to leave Bellingham before that time."

"No," Sarah said, a slight catch in her throat. "I had not planned to leave."

Chapter Fifteen

Sarah's emotions were as taut as a newly wound clock, so she dared not work for fear of ruining some masterpiece. At the same time, she could not sit still. After leaving Sir Harold and the runner in the book room, she decided that she needed exercise to smooth the sharp edges off her emotions and fresh air to clear her head.

With the sun beaming down as warm as a summer's day in London, she did not go upstairs for a wrap, but slipped out the rear entrance and walked toward the stables, the heels of her half boots making little clicking sounds on the cobbled path.

When she had come outside, she had had no set destination in mind, but as she neared the stables, she knew exactly where she wanted to go, to the waterfall.

As she had done when Matthew was with her, she took the path that wound downward from behind the stables, keeping up a brisk pace through the spruce forest, then veering right when the path split. As the spruce became less dense, she spied the dark green ferns she had remarked before and the carpet of deep blue gentians. This time she felt an affinity for the brave little flower that managed to survive amid this wild, majestic country, for she, too, had survived.

At least, she had survived Angus Newsome's machinations. Now she had to wonder if she would survive a broken heart. When it came time to leave

Matthew, when she was obliged to go away from this lovely land and the man she loved, would she be brave enough, strong enough to do so?

I will, of course, she thought, her throat tight with unshed tears. *I must! But I shall always remember this beautiful place, for it is Matthew's favorite, and he shared it with me.*

From somewhere behind her Sarah thought she heard the loud, clear whistle of a curlew. No, not a curlew, some other bird, one she could not identify.

Cupping her hands above her eyes to shield them from the sun, she looked all about in the sky, trying to discover the winged creature. "Where are you, little bird? Are you lonely? Come down close to me, for I am more lonely than I can say."

"And why is that?"

"Matthew!"

Turning quickly, Sarah looked up the hillside and saw Matthew coming toward her, slipping and sliding down the rough terrain to the path.

"Matthew!" she shouted when he tripped on an exposed tree root and nearly pitched forward. "Careful of your shoulder. Why did you not take the path?"

"Since you did not tell me you were going, I was obliged to take a shortcut to catch you up."

"The bird?" she said. "Was that you?"

"Never mind the bird. Answer my question. Why are you lonely?"

She had not the will to dissemble; not here, not in this special place. "Because in a few days I will be leaving Donmore Hall."

Matthew's eyes narrowed, the gray turning dark as pewter. "What is this, madam? You cannot mean to quit before your work is done. I had thought better of you. If you leave, where am I to find another art restorer?"

Sarah did not know what to think. Was he teasing

her? Surely not. Matthew would not—could not—be so unkind.

His wanting to send her away was nothing new; he had been trying to send her away from the first moment she arrived at Donmore Hall. But this time was different. After all they had been through, she had thought . . . No! It did not matter what she thought! He had made it quite plain two nights ago, when she had kissed him, that she meant nothing to him. He had phrased it politely, saying that nothing could come of their friendship, but what he meant was that she was his employee, and when he married, his bride would be a lady.

"Is your decision to leave irrevocable?" he said. "Is there nothing I can say to change your mind?"

Thoroughly frustrated, Sarah said, "Matthew Donaldson, if you do not wish me to go, then why are you sending me away?"

"I? Send you away?" He shook his head. "I *should* do so, of course, but I cannot. I am not brave enough."

This last Sarah knew to be untrue. "You are the bravest man I know. And," she added, "the kindest."

As if he could not stop himself, he reached out with his free hand and touched her face. "Sweet Sarah, if I were kind, I would not be here. If I were kind, I would not do *this*." He stepped closer, then he slipped his hand around to the back of her head and bent down until their faces were almost touching. Then his lips found hers.

Sarah closed her eyes, giving herself up to the joy of being with the man she loved, allowing herself this one last moment of joy before she said her farewells. This was what she wanted, what she needed; a kiss so sweet, so wonderful she thought her heart would break with the beauty of it.

"My lovely Sarah," he murmured against her lips. "I know I am not worthy of someone like you. You are so sweet, so unsullied, and you deserve a far better man than me. But, I beg of you, do not go, my love."

I beg of you?

Sarah's heart felt as though it had come to a sudden stop, then it began to beat furiously. She could not believe she had heard him correctly. He had called her his love, and he said that *he* was not worthy of *her*? He who was so handsome, so sought after. A man who could have his choice of high-born ladies.

"I . . . I hardly know what to say. If not you, what kind of man do you think I deserve?"

"Someone who would not dream of living the kind of life I have led. I spoke the truth when first we met, I am no gentleman."

She put her finger across his lips. "Do not say that, for it is not true. You are the gentlest man I have ever known. And I could not ask for one who suited me more perfectly. Nor one I loved more."

As if bemused, he stared at her, then his eyes filled with such love, such wonder, that Sarah began to tremble. "Say that again," he said.

Sarah smiled, for she was feeling better by the minute. So secure, in fact, that she dared tease him a little herself. "Repeat the part about you, my beloved coxcomb? Or just the part about me loving you?"

"Minx," he said. "You know what I want to hear."

"I love you," she said, then she lifted her face again, offering him her lips.

He bent his head as if to accept the offer, but before he claimed her lips, he hesitated, his eyebrow raised as if puzzled about something. "Wait just a minute," he said. "If you love me, then why did you say you were leaving?"

"I do not want to. I never wanted to. It was your idea."

"Mine! Never!"

"When Lady Worthing suggested that I needed a

chaperon, you said it was unnecessary because I would be leaving Donmore in another few days."

He muttered a word she chose to ignore. "And how can you possibly know what I said to Lady Worthing?"

"Morag overheard . . ." She stopped, not wanting to get the maid in trouble.

He looked as if he would like to throttle someone. "Those who have nothing better to do than eavesdrop would do well to listen more carefully. I told her ladyship that you did not need a chaperon because *I* would be leaving in another few days."

"You? I do not understand. Where are you going?"

"To town. When Temple arrived, he brought word that the nefarious Mr. Wayford had been arrested on a charge brought by one of the art dealer's clients. All the paintings in his art gallery have been confiscated, and I am to see if I can identify the pieces missing from the Donaldson collection."

Happy to know he had never meant to send her away, she asked how long he would be gone.

"Once the business with the paintings is finished, I have but one other errand. A very special errand."

Since that last piece of information was accompanied by a rather satisfied smile, she could not resist asking him the nature of the errand.

"I directed a letter to your father last evening, asking if he would grant me an interview."

Bereft of speech, Sarah could only stare. He had written to her father. That could only mean . . .

"Give me a hint what I should expect, madam. Will he take pity on me, and grant my heart's desire by giving me his lovely daughter for my wife? Or will he recognize me for the disreputable creature I am and threaten me with a pistol?"

Suddenly all teasing was gone and his voice became very quiet. "What if he should say me nay?" He rubbed the back of his hand against her cheek. "What would I do without my sweet Sarah?"

"That you shall never find out, sir, for I am of age, and I say to you, yea."

Matthew could not believe the power of that one little word, and as he gazed into her warm brown eyes, so honest, so filled with love, he felt as if a whole new world had opened up for him. A world of love, the kind he had only dreamed of.

"You will be my wife?"

"Yes," she said, then she caught his hand and turned it so she could place a kiss in his palm. Her lips were soft and gentle, but they ignited a fire in him that would not be denied. When he would have gathered her in his arms, however, he realized that Newsome's bullet had made that temporarily impossible.

"Damnation!" he said. "I am finally free to take you in my arms and kiss you as I have wanted to do this age, and I am stuck with this cursed sling."

Totally frustrated, he was surprised when Sarah calmly ran her fingers down the length of the gathered white scarves. "Silk is very forgiving," she said. "Perhaps there is a way around this dilemma. There are always alternative methods."

Matthew suspected his only alternative was a swim in the icy waters beneath the falls, but he tactfully kept that observation to himself.

"You may be unaware, sir, that two key essentials of a good art restorer are patience and an eye for seeing how to fix that which seems unfixable."

"That may be so, my love, but I am no work of art."

"To me you are," she said quietly. "You are the most beautiful man I have ever known, and I want to feel your arms around me."

Matthew could only stare. Since becoming a wealthy man, he had been flattered and fawned over to a degree that would put a spaniel to the blush, but

Sarah's simple, artless compliment had touched his soul.

Not wanting to disappoint her, he said, "Do what you will, my little heart restorer."

Her cheeks turned pink with pleasure at the pun, but she made no comment. "Lift the sling outward just an inch or two," she said, "and let me show you what I have in mind."

Nothing if not cooperative, Matthew supported his injured arm with his right hand and lifted it away from his chest a few inches. "Now what?"

While he watched, fascinated by her ingenuity, Sarah ducked under the circle of his arms, and after flattening herself against his body, she wiggled her way into a standing position, totally unaware that she was driving him insane.

"How is this?" she asked, wrapping her own arms tightly around his waist. "Any pain in the shoulder?"

"No pain," he replied, his voice none too steady.

"Wonderful," she said, snuggling even closer and turning her lovely face up to his. "Now that you have me where you want me, feel free to kiss me in any way you wish."

Not needing a second invitation, Matthew Donaldson did as his art restorer suggested, to their mutual satisfaction.

PASSION RIDES THE PAST